GETTING IN WAS EASY

Rossen was through the first apron of wire as Tomanaga kept watch on the tower, his Ruger at the ready in case one of the guards turned to look at the wire or became overly curious at the muted twang of wires being cut. This was the touchiest part. They had been hesitant to shoot the guards this early in the game. Rossen snipped through a wire that sprang back, whipping him across the face, laying his cheek open to the bone. When the wire passed through his flesh, it wrapped itself around another strand, sending a singing noise through the fence. Both guards came to the side of the tower and leaned over to see what it was. Carelessly, they had left their weapons behind. Tomanaga quickly made his decision and two more *phhts* were followed by dull thuds and shuffling sounds as the men died. Each one had an extra pupil in his right eye.

THE SHOOTER

BARRY SADLER

—— THE ——
SHOOTER

A TOM DOHERTY ASSOCIATES BOOK
NEW YORK

This is a work of fiction. All the characters and events portrayed in this book are either products of the author's imagination or are used fictitiously.

THE SHOOTER

A Forge Book
Published by Tom Doherty Associates, LLC
175 Fifth Avenue
New York, NY 10010

www.tor.com

Forge® is a registered trademark of Tom Doherty Associates, LLC.

ISBN-13: 978-0-765-35796-0
ISBN-10: 0-765-35796-8

First Edition: January 1987
Second Edition: April 2007

Printed in the United States of America

0 9 8 7 6 5 4 3 2 1

Prologue

The assassin winced at the noise coming over the radio. The harsh nasal whining of some country singer saying something unintelligible about country bumpkins or pumpkins forced him to turn off the car radio.

Even though the last rays of the Tennessee sun were fading, the humidity was still high. Even with the air conditioner going full blast, circles of sweat had formed cold and clammy around his armpits as he watched the house— an old, rambling frame structure that had seen better days—on Fifteenth Avenue just off Nashville's so-called Music Row. Three days he had been watching and waiting, changing cars and location each day. The neighborhood had also seen better days; now it was primarily black and was slowly being infiltrated by Vietnamese and Cambodian refugees.

It was among them that he had waited for his target to appear. Twice he had seen him for short moments through the windows or on the porch. He could have killed him at any of those times but that was not the way it had to be done. He had to get close. The killing had to appear to be just another mugging in which the victim died.

Xuason Van Trang, former Commanding Officer of the South Vietnamese Golden Tiger Ranger regiment, had been very busy. For days he had been unable to leave his house, which also served as his HQ. From the ramshackle building he sent out orders to his agents still in Vietnam, arranging for the defection of Vietnamese political figures and for an occasional assassination. For Trang the war was far from over. He never doubted that one day he would return to his homeland to lead the fight against the communists.

The critical time for him to do so was approaching. It had taken years to establish his organization, to build a strong infrastructure from which he would be able to expand and grow inside the occupied lands of South Vietnam.

This night he would meet with two of his agents who had just returned from Singapore. Through them he would give his orders and they would arrange his transport back to the land of his birth. It was a good time. The years of preparation were beginning to pay off. His exile was almost at an end.

His car was brought around to the front of the house, driven by one of his former Rangers. Climbing into the back seat, he greeted his driver, *"Cam on ong."*

Houng Shiu, who now served as his chauffeur and bodyguard, was a former paratroop sergeant major, a tough, wiry little man with quick hands and eyes. Those eyes had grown less cautious with the passing of years, however. He did not notice the nondescript vehicle following him as he drove his commander to the meeting at the Golden Pagoda restaurant on Nineteenth Avenue. He waited in the car in the parking lot as Colonel Trang entered the restaurant. He stayed behind as a matter of security. Not even he was to know the faces of those Trang was meeting. What he did not know he could not speak.

Parking his car where he could see the chauffeur and the entrance to the Golden Pagoda, the assassin waited. Patience and timing were everything. He had no interest in those whom Colonel Trang was meeting; the man was his sole objective. He climbed out of his car easily; with the settling of night he felt better. There was always something comforting about shadows. They were good, soothing to the senses. From the back seat he took a straw cowboy hat, settling it uncomfortably on his head. The wide brim concealed his features in the dark. Jeans and a Levi's jacket completed his camouflage. To any casual eye he would appear to be just another of those would-be singers or cowboys who wandered the streets of Nashville. He would not let anyone get close enough to see his face. He was ready.

Walking casually across the parking lot, he neared the car. Coming at it from the rear, he kept out of sight of the rearview and side mirrors as long as he could, letting his body move naturally; nothing in his motions would show concern or intent that could be transmitted through a nervous or hasty gesture.

Through his side mirror Shiu caught a quick glimpse of the thin figure in jeans and wide-brimmed cowboy hat. He had thought about getting himself one. They had more style than the dark blue golf cap he normally wore. Yes, he would get one someday and it would be a

Stetson, too. Automatically, he began to turn his head to take a look. He never finished. His head slumped forward to rest on the steering wheel.

Smoothly, the cowboy opened the door and slid Shiu over until he slumped on the floor on the passenger side. Adjusting his tan pigskin gloves, he removed a clean red handkerchief from his back pocket. The cowboy fastidiously wiped the shiny silver spike clean of the few drops of blood which had adhered to it after entering Shiu's ear for a length of six inches.

Taking his hat off, he exchanged it for the blue golf cap and prepared for his wait. The sun had set, the shadows already growing long and dark. Lighting a cigarette, he leaned back into the cushion and relaxed. So far this was going very well, very well indeed. This time he would give himself a special treat and indulge in a layover in San Francisco before going home. He liked San Francisco, especially Chinatown. In his mind he sang a song as he waited. *Ta mong non song song tran chien Bein, Tu lai ne chien me Qua . . .*

He didn't finish. The square shoulders of Colonel Trang appeared at the ornate doors of the Golden Pagoda.

Trang motioned for his car to pick him up. Putting out the cigarette, the assassin started the motor. He moved the car out slowly, taking it to the outside of the covered driveway where the light was dim.

A bit irritably, Trang crossed over to the car, not even wondering why his driver had not come closer to the door.

Opening the rear door, he leaned forward to enter. His eyes came up to meet those of the driver. "Who . . ." His question was terminated by the soft mercury-cored .380 bullet entering his forehead. The car interior absorbed most of the sound of the shot. Cowboy helped the Colonel's forward fall with his hand, pulling him to the back seat, then reached over to close the door. Dropping the gun by the Colonel's body, he retrieved his own hat. He backed up, putting the car back in the parking lot.

He went to his own car, pulled smoothly out, and headed over to West End, where he turned right and hit the interstate taking him to the airport, humming the last verse to his song as he drove. *Tien Buc, tien Buc, tiem ngai nha toung, Toi xe le Quan Nhan dien xe Vietnam.*

Turning his car in at the Avis rental desk, he walked down the row of airline counters until he found what he wanted: a plane leaving in fifteen minutes for Roanoke, Virginia. That would do. Once in Roanoke he would take another plane to San Francisco. Paying his fare in cash, he went up the escalator to the upper level, dropping the silver spike into a trash can on his way. He was very content this had gone quite well. Cao Lam Phang would be pleased, but then he was always pleased. Never had he failed in one of his assignments. He was, as Comrade Colonel Cao Lam Phang had often said, "quite gifted."

--------------------------------- One

Sweat beaded up under his eyes. Strain was beginning to tell. Too many hours of waiting, watching. The street below was quiet now. The gunfire had faded away to a few sporadic bursts somewhere out of sight. The tanks and armored cars which had moved into the city during the night and surrounded the Presidential Palace had reduced opposition to no more than a nuisance factor.

Rossen had known of the coup two weeks in advance. Not the exact time, but close enough for him to wait for it to come down. That's just what he had done: sat in the hotel room for two weeks, going out only for short spells to get food and keep the help from becoming too suspicious of a foreigner who always stayed in his room.

Wiping the salt irritant from his eyes, he scoped out the street once more, taking special note of sites across the Avenida de la Revolución where countersnipers would most probably be placed to provide security for the new junta when they arrived.

His room was in the corner where it faced out to the steps of the palace. Not many would think of it as a shooting platform. The range was six hundred and thirty meters to the doors of the palace.

Tomanaga was set up in a vacant office on the other side of the street. To communicate they used commercial walkie-talkies. No dialogue went on between them. Instead they used a series of clicks on the radios to send messages. When they made the hit, Tomanaga was to provide a distraction to cover their escape.

Two weeks. God, it seemed like he'd been waiting two months. When he'd been contacted for the job, he almost passed on it. There were just too many obstacles and he had to make sure of the target: Jorge María Guzmán.

Poliltics in Central and South America is like trying to do Chinese calculus using Roman numerals. Hard as hell to figure anything out. He and Tommy had come to an understanding long ago. Whenever they took a job like this, the target had to need killing, and in this neck of the woods that meant they had a lot of job opportunities. But Guzmán was definitely very high on the list of those who needed to have their allotted time on earth cut as short as possible.

He had used the services of one of his friends in the Company for a profile readout on Guzmán before accepting the contract. In fact, his friend, former Sergeant Major Virden, now a Company station officer in Costa Rica, had led him to believe that the Company and State Department would consider the termination of Jorge Guzmán a definite plus.

Jorge María Guzmán:
Born Buenos Aires 3 Dec. 1938.
Educated at Harvard and University of Moscow.
Close friends with Fidel Castro and Daniel Ortega of Nicaragua.
Ties with several terrorist organizations, including Black September, PLO, and the Bader-Meinhof Gang.

Suspected of direct participation in fourteen terrorist attacks.

Specialist in gaining the support of key personnel of vulnerable governments or new movements of liberation by either buying them, blackmailing them, or proving to them that they and their families would suffer terribly if they did not come around.

One of the terrorist charges against him was that he had personally killed the wife and five children of a mayor in Bolivia by dousing the entire family in gasoline and setting them on fire. The youngest child was three months old.

This was his target. Señor Guzmán would be with the junta party when they arrived to protect his investments. He had the hammer on at least two key members of the junta. Through them he would try and turn the coup around by infiltrating it with personnel of his choice, as had been done with the Sandinista movement in Nicaragua. With him out of the picture, the new government might have a chance to stabilize.

Rossen had been given reason enough to waste the piece of shit.

Through the scope, he watched flights of pigeons being disturbed by the passage of a convoy of military vehicles. His eyes watered. He raised the ART to the roof of the palace.

Now he knew it was close. Six men had moved to the roof, taking up sites on all sides. Four men with scoped rifles and two with light machine guns. Across the avenue were others; he had counted fourteen different positions with armed men on them. They wouldn't be a problem. There was little likelihood that many of them were good enough to react fast enough to scope on him and make a shot before he was out of the room.

It was approaching noon, and the streets were as bare as they had been during the night. Martial law had been declared. Anyone found on the streets was subject to arrest. Anyone who ran would be shot without question. Wisely, the city's inhabitants stayed in their homes.

He laughed, remembering a time that he'd been picked up when martial law had been declared during another coup.

He and Tomanaga were in the room at the Prado when the tanks had moved in. It was stupid, but he'd gone outside the next morning and stood in front of the hotel. He thought no one would pay any attention to him. No such luck!

A weapons carrier filled with troops came by. The sergeant in charge had stopped in front of him, called him over, and demanded his papers. Rossen showed him his passport and was told to get in the back with the troops to be taken to a detention center till he could be checked out. From their shoulder insignia, Rossen knew who their comandante was, Colonel Morales. He had arranged in the last month for the Colonel to get some equipment that he desperately needed. To the sergeant he had said, "Call Comandante Morales and tell him you have me in custody. I am an amigo of his."

The sergeant didn't think the Comandante had any gringo friends but he couldn't take a chance. *"Bueno"* was all he replied.

They drove him to the city soccer stadium. More than a thousand detainees were milling about. The stadium had been divided into several sectors by barbed wire. Women and children in one, the men divided into several others. Rossen guessed they had been separated according to their status or degree of suspicion.

The one they placed him in had about twenty foreigners. Some Germans, Italians, others. A mixed bag. Among them were three American TV journalists. This had been their first time out of the States and none of them spoke a word of Spanish. Rossen knew that they were not going to be hurt and neither was he. They were just being held until their identity could be confirmed, but they didn't know that. All of them had pale green looks to them, especially around the eyes and the corners of their mouths. He guessed it was because every few minutes a detachment of soldiers would go into one of the sectors and call out a few names, place the men between the guards, and march them out of the stadium, and then in a minute or two would come a burst of machine-gun fire.

He knew it would take some time before they'd be able to reach Colonel Morales; he was probably very busy at this time. Going up to one of the guards, he spoke in Spanish and handed over two American twenty-dollar bills and waited by the wire until the guard came back, about twenty minutes later. When he returned he was carrying a bottle of Johnnie Walker Red. Taking the bottle through the wire, Rossen handed him a ten and went back to the center of the sector.

One of the reporters came over to him, voice quivering with the effort to control his fear.

"What's going to happen to us, do you think?"

Cracking open the bottle, Rossen took a long pull. He watched another detachment take four men out and march them around the corner. When the machine-gun fire died down, he looked up at the sun, took another drink, and said, "Well, at this rate I'd guess they'll probably get to us around two or three."

"You mean they're going to . . ." The young American couldn't finish saying it, so Rossen did it for him.

"Shoot us? That's exactly right. We're going up against the wall."

All three of the reporters crowded around him, shock clearly inscribed in their faces and actions. "They can't do that," they protested.

Rossen grunted, "Tell them, not me. They're the ones with the machine guns!"

Frantically, another reporter began to sob. "But what are we going to do?" Rossen moved away from them toward the side of the stadium where there was more shade. "I don't know about you, but I'm going to try and finish the jug first."

He left them in a huddle, heads together, trying to figure out some way to interdict their impending fate. To avoid cracking up, Rossen took another drink.

It was nearly two before the sergeant who had picked him up returned with six troops as an escort. He marched up to Rossen, still sitting in the shade.

"Señor Rossen, you will come with us, please," he said in Spanish.

Rossen hauled himself to his feet, stepped

in the center of the escort, and did a smart about-face. The reporters were aghast. He had about a quarter of his bottle left. Tossing it to one of them, he yelled out, "Have a drink on me. I'll see you in hell in about half an hour. You're next!"

The escort took him outside the stadium to a waiting army limousine which returned him to his hotel with the warning to be certain to stay off the streets for the next couple of days. When they pulled away from the stadium, a rattle of machine-gun fire followed them. He knew that the terrified reporters thought it had been him being shot and they were next.

Tommy cracked up when he told him what had come down. "I bet when those guys were released, they never even bothered to pack. Just took the next plane out to go home and look for some other kind of work."

The grinding of tank treads brought him back to the job at hand. Another tank had pulled up to join the other two. That gave one on each flank and one centered on the broad marble steps leading up to the main entrance of the palace. There were also two armored cars and a half-dozen jeeps with .30-caliber machine guns mounted on them covering all avenues of access and egress. Between them were smartly turned-out troops in full battle gear. The new bosses weren't taking many chances. He had figured that, which was one of the reasons for taking up the site he now held, the distance. There just weren't that many shooters in the world who could be counted on to make a kill at that kind of range.

The lesser, more refined drone of car motors came next. The tank had been taking point.

Two more jeeps and four motorcycles came in next, then the target. If his info was right, Guzmán would be in the second vehicle. There were three cars in the caravan: two Cadillacs and a Mercedes limousine.

That would be it. The Mercedes was in number two position. He didn't need communications with Tommy to know he'd be on the job. They'd worked too many times together in the past. Tommy was always where he was supposed to be.

Tomanaga used his steel hook to move the venetian blinds apart. The window was already cracked about a foot. More than enough. He wasn't there to make any kills, just add to the confusion.

Taking a deep breath, Rossen let the barrel of the M-14 rest on the window ledge, the Psionics sound suppressor giving it an ungainly exaggerated look. Through the scope he brought the car into focus. He would wait until the target was in the clear. If at all possible, he wasn't to take out anyone else. Just Guzmán.

From the first car men began to exit, climbing the stairs to the seat of power. Several were in uniform and they talked as they climbed. Rossen hit the walkie-talkie button with two series of three clicks, receiving a two-click series. Tomanaga was alerted.

The door to the Mercedes opened, and suddenly Rossen had the back of Guzmán's head in his scope lens with his finger taking the trigger slack up until less than a hundredth pound pressure remained. He let off a skosh. The man in his scope was bald. Guzmán had a full head of thick brown hair. The bald man waited for the rest of the car to unload. Guzmán was last. Rossen couldn't pull one off because the man never got in the clear.

They followed the first party up the flight of stairs. Guzmán stayed in the center of them. Once he could have taken him, but the round would have probably gone on through and killed the bald man as well. Rossen's hand began to tremble with nervous tension. Goddamn it to hell, when would he step clear?

Taking a deep breath, he let it out slowly to control the tremble and regain his composure. Calmly, easily, gently, that's the ticket.

Don't rush it. Take your time. The moment would come if he was ready for it.

The army troops on guard were visibly agitated. Officers kept yelling and gesturing to them to keep on the alert.

The target was almost to the top of the stairs. If Guzmán got inside the doors, then he'd have to wait until they came back out. That could take hours, if not days. Too long. He wasn't going to hang around much longer.

Guzmán moved to the top of the stairs. An army officer called to him from below. Through the scope he turned in slow motion. Rossen filled the scope with his body, moving till Guzmán's face was centered. A quick mental adjustment, breath control, inhaling, letting out half of it, finger taking up trigger slack, all automatic responses. If you had to think about it, you were too late.

Two

Guzmán's lips moved as he spoke to the Colonel standing below him. His face turned slightly. In the scope he was looking straight into the eye of Rossen.

The last thousandths of a pound of pressure were taken up. The rifle rode back against his shoulder once, twice. Guzmán's face assumed a vacuous expression for a split second, then the back of his head erupted, blowing brains and blood all the way to the door, scattering tissue all over the men around him. The next round took him in mid-chest. Rossen didn't have to wait and see to know the damage done. A 173-grain soft-nosed slug traveling at 2,550 feet per second would turn everything inside the chest cavity into black jelly.

Guzmán was down and dead before Tomanaga got off his round. The vintage M-79 grenade launcher sent one round of HE into the side of the palace to explode harmlessly against the stone wall. Another, also placed where it could do no harm, entered the window of an abandoned store, scattering glass and debris onto the street. Two more rounds and the square was in a panic.

The junta members were quickly hustled into the safety of the palace behind a shield of soldiers. Not knowing where the fire was coming from, the troops on the square and rooftops began to fire at random, spraying all the windows in sight. The tanks joined in sending round after round into the surrounding buildings. Smoke and flame began covering the square.

Leaving the M-14 in the room, Rossen was out the door before the first soldier got off a round. Heading to the rear of the hotel, he climbed out the window to the fire escape; moving quickly but carefully, he climbed down the rusted, rickety steel ladder to the street.

From the first shot to his feet hitting the deck was less than forty-five seconds.

Moving quickly but not running, he turned the corner taking a block south from the Avenida de la Revolución. From his pocket he took a key to unlock the padlock on the tin door of a carport. Pushing the door fully open, he climbed into the Toyota Landcruiser and started the vehicle, heading out back onto the street. Turning west on Calle Doce, sounds of cannon and machine-gun fire followed him.

If Tomanaga was on time, he should be waiting at the intersection of Calle Veinte and Avenida de la Cruces by the corner of Lloyds Bank. The time it took to travel the eight blocks seemed incredibly long. Time was on his back. Seconds were crucial. By now the word was out. Soldiers from the capital garrison would be cordoning off the city, blocking all roads in and out. The airport was already closed. Time was the hammer now. He slowed down, not stopping. Where was Tommy? The door opened and the nisei grabbed the dash handle with his stainless-steel claw to pull himself in.

"It's done. Let's get the fuck out of here while we still can."

Rossen needed no further encouragement. Right now they would stand out like Zulus on an iceberg.

Tomanaga reached into the back seat, and from under a blanket he pulled out an AK-47, checked the mag and the action, chambered a round, and kept an eye on the back. Sirens began to wail. No one was on the streets. The people had enough experience to know there was only one thing to do when the military hit the streets looking for terrorists. That was to stay inside out of sight and pray that no member of their own family had been involved in whatever had taken place.

Rossen drove to another carport, part of a deserted building which had once housed a radio station. They headed up the stairs to the roof and crossed over the roofs of three buildings. So far so good. Everything was going as it was supposed to. On the third building they entered the unlocked roof door and climbed down to the bottom floor. There they would wait until dark, then they would have to make their way to the outskirts of the city avoiding patrols and the *guardia*.

Rossen had to give the contractor credit for setting things up right. If the rest of the operation went as smoothly, by midnight they would be out of the country and on their way back stateside. Stateside? It seemed that was something he was forever doing: trying to go home, and it was useless. He watched the nisei from the corner of his eye. Tomanaga placed himself where he could keep an eye on the two doors leading to their temporary shelter.

Tomanaga, the man with the steel hand. It was hard for him to remember when Tommy didn't have the claw on his left wrist. Tomanaga caught his glance and smiled at him as if to say, "I know. You're my brother, too." They *were* brothers. Stronger than any bonds of birth was the bond of blood; blood from uncounted firefights and killings where each depended on the other for survival, knowing that either would give up his life without hesitation if it would save the other.

They had hoped after the job in Honduras last year that they would have been able to get out of the business, but it hadn't worked that way. They had tried to go straight in Guatemala. It hadn't taken long for them to find out that in the business world they were stone cherries. They got busted out in less than six months. Now they were back at it. Perhaps it was better this way. One day they would go out and not come back. That, too, was expected. Natural.

Outside, traffic had picked up. The *ejército* was out in force, patrolling the streets. Rossen would not have liked being on a list of suspected dissidents this day. He knew that all over the city, doors were being kicked down and people dragged out for questioning. That was the bad part. He didn't like getting civilians involved with their game plans, but the contractor had promised to make it known as soon as they were out of the country that Guzmán had been their only target and why. Perhaps that would end the manhunt.

Tomanaga whispered to him, "Check the broom closet."

Rossen opened the door to the closet. Inside were supplies: food and water, a couple of blankets, and peasant clothes—well-used garments which still carried the odor of their former owners and probably some little blood-sucking creatures living in the seams as well.

"Hey, Tomanaga, let's wait to change clothes."

There was no argument on that.

For the next eight hours they waited. Long, boring, tense hours. Twice the front door to the building they were hiding in was shaken by patrolling *guardia*. When the shadows grew long on the streets, they changed into the *campesino* garments, hid their weapons under the loose folds of a poncho, put on straw sombreros to keep their faces in the shadows, and left by the back door. Three times before the hit came down they had rehearsed the route and the time it would take to reach the rendezvous point. Rossen hoped that they wouldn't have to blow anybody's shit away getting there.

They had done their job; any more killing was a waste.

Weaving their way through deserted streets and alleys to the outskirts of the city, they managed to avoid all patrols by staying to the shadows until they hit a field of cane, plunged into it, and kept moving. So far so good. On the other side of the field was where they would find their transport waiting for them in an old hangar. A C-47 used for crop spraying was supposed to be standing by.

By the time they reached the dirt strip, their *campesino* clothes were stuck to their backs, their chests laboring as anxiety ate at them and fear made them question every shadow and sound. Would the plane be there? Had they been double-crossed? They lay down at the edge of the dirt runway; this was no time to get careless. Carefully, they checked out the area. No sign of government troops or *guardia* patrols. From the hangar there was only darkness, not a light to be seen. That didn't bother them. It was natural. Still, Rossen wished they knew for certain that their plane and pilot would be waiting for them.

Weapons at the ready, they kept about thirty feet apart. Rossen led slightly, Tomanaga giving cover, then Rossen doing the same for him. They crossed the last terribly long open space to reach the shadows of the ramshackle hangar.

"Took you guys long enough."

The words nearly made them jump out of their skins. They swung around ready to fire, fingers on triggers.

"Put those damn things away. They make me nervous." Coming closer to them, the small blond man identified himself only as, "I'm your pilot and that's all you need to know and I don't want to know anything about you."

Rossen grunted back, "Good enough. Now what?"

The pilot, obviously another gringo, grinned in the dark. "Well, it would help if you would give me a hand and let's get the hangar doors open and then I'll do my best to get your asses out of this country before they hang us all out to dry."

Tomanaga kept watch as the pilot and Rossen pushed open the tin doors. To the east, the sun was breaking. It was startling how suddenly the dawn came. One moment there was nothing but heavy, humid black, then the stark outlines of ten-thousand-foot volcanoes framed in gold and red.

"Okay, you guys. Keep your eyes open till I get my crate warmed up."

Tomanaga took the left side of the hangar, Rossen the other. Staying to the darker shad-

ows, they listened. The quiet was deafening.
Inside the hangar they heard one engine cough,
miss, then catch, and then the one came on-
line. The roar settled down to a smoother
throb. Easing off the brakes, the pilot moved
the old crate out of the hangar. Leaning out of
the cockpit, he yelled out over the drone of
the engines, "Well? Are you guys going with
me or not?"

Tomanaga climbed in first, keeping watch
from the door until Rossen was safely on board.

Not wasting any time, the pilot put the brakes
back on, built up revs to the red line, released
them, and turned down the dirt strip. Slowly
the old plane began to rise. When its wheels
came off the ground, the men in the back felt
as if their guts had drained out of their asses.
It was the release of tension. They were off.
For once things had gone down the way they
were supposed to.

Closing the door, Rossen and Tomanaga
moved to sit down on canvas seats. From the
window Rossen could see the lights of the city
sparkling in the clear morning air. One side of
the world was dark, one red and gold. Climbing to eleven thousand, the plane leveled off,
engines humming smoothly. Rossen put his
forehead against the window. The coolness
was good; even the vibration being transmitted through the frame of the forty-year-old

aircraft was comforting. Moving his head back from the window, he looked over at Tommy. He was already asleep. Good man, good friend.

They would be in the air for a few hours. The first leg of the flight would take them to a strip a few miles off the coast of Belize. Until then there was nothing more to do. He closed his eyes, leaving the pilot to do his job and guide the plane through the morning skies. Now that they were airborne there was little chance that anything would go wrong. He knew the pilot would be heading out to sea, flying along the coast. No problem. Most of the countries in Latin America only had radar around major cities, and there were none on the flight path.

Hydraulics lowering the landing gear opened his and Tommy's eyes at the same time. They were coming down. The earth below had changed shape. Low rolling hills were covered with jungle and stretched to the west as far as the eye could see. To the east was an eye-piercing expanse of ocean.

Setting the plane down on a strip that had once served a now defunct lumber company, the pilot rolled them to a smooth stop. He didn't cut the motors. Sticking his head out so he could see down the aisle, he shouted,

"All right, you guys. Get the fuck out of here. I got some other things to do today."

From his window, Rossen could see Juliano waiting for them. That was good. He liked the man. They had worked together in the past. If it hadn't been for him, they wouldn't have taken this job, or had much faith in it.

"Okay, Tommy. Let's get out of here and let that sour-tempered son of a bitch go about his business."

Opening the door, they didn't lower the ladder but just hopped down.

"I'm glad to see you again, *compañeros*, and know that all has gone well," Juliano greeted them.

Tomanaga nodded his head in agreement. "You aren't the only one."

By the time Juliano had escorted them to a waiting car, the pilot had turned the C-47 around and was heading down the strip.

Sardonically, Rossen commented, "He's a busy little thing, isn't he?"

Juliano laughed as he opened the car trunk. "Don't mind him. He's all right and he is always where he is supposed to be. That is not a small thing." They had to agree.

Taking their weapons from them, Juliano put them in the trunk and took out a suitcase. "Here are your clothes and your passports. As far as the rest of the world knows, you have been in Belize fishing for the last two weeks. By this afternoon you will be back in the States."

Changing out of their rags into their own clothes made them feel better. More like themselves.

Climbing into the car, Juliano drove down the old logging road to where he could connect with the road taking them into Belize City.

To Tommy he said, "In the back seat are some sandwiches and soft drinks if you want them."

Tomanaga shook his head in the negative. "No thanks, Juliano. I'm still a bit tired. Just wake me when I get back to the States."

Juliano and Rossen drove on with Tomanaga climbing over into the back seat to stretch out.

Looking around him, Juliano shook his head. "You know that strip we just landed on?"

Rossen nodded.

"Well, last night it was used by some other gentlemen to bring in arms for the guerrillas in Guatemala. The gentlemen there are taking a lesson from Colombia. Trading drugs for weapons."

Rossen wasn't surprised. There was little that could be done to stop the influx of arms into Central America. The local governments didn't have the money or equipment to deal with it. If he and Tommy could fly in with no problems, then so could the other side.

Juliano steered around a tree stump. "One of these days I think we are going to have to put a crimp in those gentlemen's plans." He left the statement hanging. Rossen knew what he was up to and refused to take the bait.

Juliano cast it out again.

"Don't you think it would be a good idea?"

Wearily, Rossen grumbled at him, "Just say it, Juliano, and stop this bullshit. I'm too tired for it. What do you want?"

Clearing his throat, the latino spat an oyster out of the open window. "We are considering giving the local governments a little help. We can't buy radar for them, but if a few of the brains on both sides of the dope and gun deals were to come to a sudden and violent end, it might slow things up a bit."

Rossen shook his head violently from side to side. "No you don't! You sneaky little son of a bitch. Me and Tomanaga are going home. So knock it off and don't bother trying to appeal to my patriotism. It just doesn't work."

Juliano smiled at nothing. "Okay, Señor Shooter. If that's the way you feel, we will leave it alone"—he paused—"for now."

——————Three

Juliano took them straight to the airport, letting them out in front of the dingy terminal. He went to the rear of the car, opened the trunk, and took out their bags. Handing them their tickets, he smiled slyly. "Think about what I said, amigos. I think you will have a change of heart. You always have. You two dinosaurs can't help yourselves. You still think there is right and wrong in the world. Obviously a flaw in your characters."

Tomanaga took his bag and pointed his claw

menacingly. "Go fuck yourself, Juliano. You ain't getting us this time. We have enough money to take it easy for a while."

Juliano laughed pleasantly. "That's what you said last time." He went to each of them, giving them a Latin *embrazo*. "Take care of yourselves, my friends. Remember, go for *la vida pura*, the pure life."

"You too, compadre." Rossen left him with that. He and Tomanaga checked in at the counter, cleared immigration, and headed for gate 3. Mexicana Air would take them to Mérida in Yucatán, from there a flight to New Orleans, then home. They would be back at the mountain by midnight.

At LA International they took a cab to a friend's trailer in Tarzana. Another retired warhorse, Cappy had once been the CO of the Halo Committee at Fort Bragg. He'd slid thorugh Nam clean, then took his retirement, went back over working for the Company, and caught a round through the elbow that took his forearm off.

He and Tomanaga liked to share hook stories. He never asked where they were going or what they were doing; he'd been around too long for that. But if they ever needed a place to get messages or leave a vehicle, or just somewhere to crash for a while, the door was always open. He was a good man whose life had gone and left him with nothing but the cold memories of the past to sustain him.

Cappy wasn't in when they got there. Rossen left a note on the trailer door, saying they'd picked up the car and would call him in a couple of days. Cappy could have been anyplace. He supplemented his pension and fought boredom by writing articles for men's adventure magazines. Sometimes he'd get a job that would take him out of the country. Once he'd called them from Tegucigalpa, Honduras, when he and Tomanaga were in Guatemala City, saying he was in the hospital and on his way back home after falling off a mountaintop while doing a story on the Miskito Indians. He had broken his leg, multiple fractures.

Rossen knew that Cappy wished he could have gone with them on some jobs, and if he'd been able to, he was one of the very few they would have wanted to take. If Juliano thought they were dinosaurs, he should have met Cappy and Colonel Oates. When those two got together, World War II was nothing more than a minor incident.

Rossen drove, taking them out of the city and past March Air Force Base at Riverside, and up onto the mountain. The past year they'd made their base at a small resort town called Idlewild, where the high mountain air was a welcome relief from the constant smog that lay over Los Angeles like a case of chronic halitosis.

Idlewild served their needs perfectly. Close enough to the city that they could get to a major airport in a couple of hours and still far enough out of the way that they weren't bothered by bullshit calls and drop-ins. The town minded its own business, the residents staying to ·themselves, satisfied if their more casual neighbors never made an appearance. They were left alone.

The only real contact they had there was with Pappy's war-stories buddy, Lieutenant Colonel Leonard Oates, U.S. Army Retired. Colonel Oates was a hard-nosed, dyed-in-the-wool, old-time patriot who worked at it with a passion. He was involved with anything and everything that had to do with the military and soldiering. His main passion for the last five years was MIAs in Vietnam and Laos. He firmly believed that American soldiers were still being held there by the enemy.

He'd brought Rossen and Tomanaga up to the mountain to help run a couple of shooting courses. The Colonel ran a paramilitary training center where he'd instruct police and private individuals in everything from rapelling—which he loved—to executive protection and survival. He kept only three men on regular payroll; the rest, like Rossen and Tommy, were contracted for when he had a class come in.

Their cabin was near Oates's, on the north side of town. A dirt road ran to it past four other cabins owned by the Colonel for his instructors and visitors. Each sat in its own grove of ponderosa pines.

When they opened the door, the cabin smelled musty, unlived in. Tomanaga wrinkled his nose and moved across the room to open the windows.

Rossen dropped his bag. He thought about calling the Colonel to let him know they were in but decided against it. They'd call in the morning. All he wanted now was to put it down and crash for ten hours. Lately there was a feeling of disorientation when they made a jump like this. Sometimes it seemed incredible that in such a short time they could come so far, go to and leave a world of revolutions and death, of plots and counterplots, of assassinations and terrorism, and all of it just a few hours from the cool comfort of their small mountain log cabin.

Pulling back the covers on his bed, Rossen slid in between sheets that smelled of mold and damp. It didn't matter. It was good to just lie back, close your eyes, and sleep the deep sleep of exhaustion, to let nerves relax and settle. One deep breath. He held it a moment—as he would if he were taking up trigger slack before a shot—and let it out very slowly. Before the breath was completed he was asleep.

Tomanaga gave the cabin a quick check-over, then took his hook off and set it on the end table near his bed. The stump hurt, but then it always hurt. Flexing it free of its bindings, he felt the deep burning in the tender flesh. Lying down, he closed his eyes, but it took a moment longer for him to fall off. He had always known that he had more imagination than Rossen, and now he wondered briefly about what could come next. That something would come he never questioned. There were just too few in the world with their qualifications, and the demand was great with no sign of slacking off. Someone would come for them and they would go out again. It didn't matter how much money they made. They would go again and again, and one day they wouldn't come back. That was all right, too. It was the way it was supposed to be and he wouldn't change it if he could. He tried to recall a line from an old song, something about a disputed barricade and rendezvous. Then he slept, the pain in his wrist distant but waiting.

"Get your asses up in there. You going to sleep all day? Move it out, you slugs!"

Rossen opened sticky eyes, his head aching.

"My God," he moaned, "what is that? A castrated water buffalo?"

Tomanaga also winced at the grating voice. "Come on in, Colonel, you got a key."

Oates unlocked the door and plunged inside, going straight to Rossen's bedroom. Forcing one eye open all the way, Rossen wished he hadn't. There was something wrong about a man in his seventies having so much energy. It always made him feel less than adequate. Oates stood like the statue of the ultimate warrior: feet spread, hands on his hips, starched khakis with razor creases tailored around his stocky body. He was an impressive devil with close-cropped steel-gray hair and a bristling twist-ended mustache that any British sergeant major would have envied.

"Good morning, Colonel. How's it going?"

"Don't give me that bullshit. You and Tomanaga get up; I want to talk to you about something. Take a shower and I'll put on some coffee."

Meekly, Rossen and Tomanaga obeyed. Oates was too hard to argue with. It was easier to just go ahead and do what he wanted *now*. They would do it in the end anyhow, so they just made it easier on their nerves and saved themselves a lot of browbeating.

By the time they'd followed his orders and made it into the kitchen, Oates was waiting for them, coffee poured in metal cups, mustache bristling with electric energy, blue eyes sparking. They knew they were in trouble. When the Colonel looked that good, he had something unpleasant up his sleeve.

Sitting down, they were grateful that Oates waited until they had taken their first sip of the steaming brew before beginning.

"Now, listen up! I have someone I want you to meet and talk to. He's a friend of mine and Cappy's. So show him some respect. When you came in last night, I called him at his home and told him to get his tail out here. He'll be arriving sometime this afternoon, so make yourselves presentable."

Putting his cup down, Rossen took a chance on pissing the Colonel off and asked, "Who is it you want us to see?"

Oates's mustache bristled even more fiercely. "If I had wanted you to know his name at this point, I would have told it to you. Is that clear, Sergeants Rossen and Tomanaga?"

Resigned to their abused state, they agreed that it was very clear.

"Okay, Colonel. We'll be ready." That was all they said, knowing it would be futile to try and get any more information out of the old war-horse. When he had a hair up his ass, he was impossible to reason with. Besides that they liked and respected him. His history entitled him to say damn near anything he wanted to them.

At four that afternoon they were ensconced in the living room of Oates's home. The walls were covered with photos and mementos of years past. World War II, Korea, Vietnam, plus a number of pictures and souvenirs from Thailand, Israel, Spain, Iran, and other countries where Oates had worked as an adviser in recent years.

From outside the crunch of tires on pinecones said their company was there.

Tomanaga started to get up and go to the door with Oates. He was waved back to his chair by an impatient hand.

They could hear him greeting his guest. Trying not to appear too obvious about their curiosity, they tried to peer out the open door.

A figure resembling Oates's square body came in.

Mentally, Rossen groaned. *Oh, shit!*

Former Regular Army Major Robert Green grinned at them as he entered the room, knowing the effect his appearance was having on them. He loved it.

"Good afternoon, gentlemen. My God, you two are hard to track down. Don't you ever leave a forwarding address or number? It's taken me six months to locate you."

Rising, Rossen shook his hand. "Ever think maybe we like our privacy?"

Nonplussed, Robert Green moved to the liquor cabinet, helping himself to scotch and branch water.

Oates knew what was going on in the room. These men all knew each other. Rossen was leery because Bob Green, onetime professional soldier turned magazine publisher, had tried for years to get him and Tomanaga involved in some of his projects, without success, and Green always had a project going.

Tomanaga looked at Rossen, shrugging his shoulders. With both Green and Oates involved, they knew what the subject matter was going to be.

MIAs.

Four

Green settled his frame in a well-used recliner, not saying anything more for a moment and giving Oates time to play host and set out the scotch and Jack Daniel's. Once glasses were filled, he leaned forward and rested the base of his whiskey glass on his knee.

"I would like very much for you two to listen to me for a few moments without interruption and no wise-ass bullshit." He looked from face to face. "Will you do that for me?"

Rossen and Tomanaga nodded, each taking a pull from their glasses.

Green took one last long swallow, cleared his throat, and looked at Oates, who gave him a thumbs-up sign.

"You guys know a bit about my record. Some think I'm crazy, and I don't care. I'm doing what I think is important work and it's not just publishing my magazine to make a buck. I don't need the money. We've all smelled cordite here, and have had friends and comrades die in battle. We have all been shot at and have done our share of shooting back.

"Rossen, I know that you and Tomanaga still go out on jobs and you pick the people you work for very carefully. You're soldiers whether you're in uniform or not. You can't get it out of your systems and you won't till you either die of old age or get your shit blown away. Me and the Colonel are the same way."

He lifted his glass for Oates to give him a refill.

"I don't know if you're aware of it, but I have another reason for my interest in the MIA-POW cause. First, I was taken prisoner in Korea in '52, so I know a bit about what those men are going through. Second, I had some good friends in the camps, men who saved my life, helped me to survive. Some of those men never came back and I know they were alive when the armistice was signed.

"Oates was there with me. He knows it's true."

That surprised them. They knew Oates had been taken prisoner but not that he had been in the same camp as Green. That explained a lot of things about their relationship.

Green closed his eyes as though trying to place each word where it would do the most good.

"By the living God! I know that there are Americans still being held in Southeast Asia. Because I have money and the influence of my publishing businesses, I have a lot of contacts with high-ranking military men in several Asian governments. I have had information forwarded to me that I have checked out to the smallest detail. I have a live sighting which has been confirmed by multiple sources. Out of the hundreds of reports I have gone through this one stands up to all the tests.

"Near the junction of the borders of Laos, Cambodia, and Vietnam there is a camp. At least two Americans are being held there."

His voice grew with intensity as he spoke; not rising, just growing stronger with each word.

"I want those men out of there. The American government isn't going to do it, for God knows what reasons. They have their problems, but I don't have to wait. I have the money and the contacts. What I need now is the right team to do the job."

Draining his glass, he leaned forward, locking his eyes on those of his listeners.

"I want you to go in and bring them out if they're still alive. I want those men the way I have never wanted anything in my life. I will spend every cent I have or can borrow to do it and would go with you if I thought you'd let me!"

Rossen and Tomanaga looked at each other, expressionless.

Leaning back in the chair, Green closed his eyes, visibly trying to regain control of his emotions.

Oates took over, standing by the fireplace, his eyes on the face of his old friend.

"He means it. I've seen the evidence and it's sound. Of course, we can't guarantee they'll be there now; the last report was two months old by the time we got it.

"Listen to me. I know that you and Tomanaga are not quite the same as Green and me. Maybe you think we're just mad old men still playing war games. I assure you it's much more than that. All of our adult lives we served the armed forces of this country. It was and is our life. Green and me know that men were left behind in Korea. Men we lived with, cried with. They have never come back. That is an incredible shame for our country. If there is any chance, however remote, of getting even one American out of there, it must be taken. If we can bring back just one, then maybe we'll have the strength and courage to get the others back. If just one MIA is returned, then the American people will come together in an anger and outrage not seen since Pearl Harbor and force the politicians to do that which is necessary to gain the release of the others."

He leaned back against the mantel of the fireplace. Like Green he was shaken, his hands trembling. They had never seen the Colonel when he wasn't in total control of himself.

Rossen cleared his throat awkwardly. "Look, Colonel, Green. Let me and Tomanaga talk it over. Then we'll let you know if we're interested in the job."

Green opened his eyes. "How long will that take? Every hour is crucial."

Tomanaga leaned over and whispered in Rossen's ear.

Rossen nodded. "You'll have your answer in an hour, sir."

They left Oates's house, leaving the two men alone. Taking a small, pine-needle-littered trail alongside of the house, they followed it through cool pines. It had rained recently; in small, delicate clusters, new toadstools were pushing up through the pine needles. A couple of hundred yards from the Colonel's house they sat down on a log crossing the path.

"What do you think, Tommy?"

"I don't know. The Colonel is not one given to a lot of bullshit and neither is Green. I've always wondered if there were any of our people left over there. I know you have, too. We've talked about it before."

Rossen picked up a pinecone and tossed it downhill. "Yeah, I've wondered. But from what I've heard there's still no hard evidence, or at least none that's been released to the public."

Scratching his head with his claw, Tomanaga countered: "Since when do you believe everything the government says? Just because nothing has been released doesn't mean there's nothing there. I want to find out. What the hell else do we have to do?"

He was right. Rossen knew it. He had wondered for years about it. Thinking about what it would be like to be held captive for years with no one outside knowing if you were alive or dead. Tomanaga and he had taken all the courses on MOI (methods of interrogation), both the American manner and the Russian and Asian. It covered such esoteric matters as sensory deprivation, physical torture, starvation, and sexual humiliation. All the things that could be done to find the chink in a man's armor, to get to where his strength lives and take it piece by piece away from him.

"Okay, Tommy, if they got any hard evidence, we'll try it. Happy now?"

Tomanaga's face lit up, showing two rows of neat white teeth. "You betcha, Phü Nhãm. This number-one boy very happy."

Rossen laughed. "Knock that shit off, Tommy, you're Japanese, not Chinese. C'mon, let's go tell them."

Oates and Green were standing in the center of the living room, worry written all over their faces. Tomanaga entered first, giving them a salute with his steel hook.

"This is it. Show us something hard, and we'll try. Okay?"

Oates and Green broke into face-consuming grins. Tears ran freely as tension was released, then Rossen and Tommy had their hands shaken and backs pounded until they thought about reneging on the agreement.

Green went outside to his car and removed a locked briefcase from the trunk. Returning, he handed it, and the key, over to Tomanaga.

"You men take this and go through it. I'll be staying with Oates till tomorrow afternoon. If you have any questions at any hour, call. If it's as I said, then you'll leave with me tomorrow to start the ball rolling. Agreed?"

"Okay, Bob. We'll go through the reports and get back to you. Now, if you'll excuse us, I don't know about Tomanaga, but I'm still suffering a bit from jet lag. We'll let you know tomorrow one way or the other."

"Good enough. That's all I wanted—for you to give it a fair chance."

Walking back to the cabin, they opened the door, turned on the lights, and found a place to sit with Tomanaga taking the kitchen table. Opening the case, he took out stacks of papers and files, separated a handful, and took them to Rossen, who had settled down on the couch.

A black-and-white 8-by-10 photo on the top of the pile kept Rossen's eyes open.

Two figures jumped out at him from the glossy. They were Americans. There could be no doubt about one of them: The man was well over six feet tall, a full head above the small wiry men with pith helmets and AK-47s standing to either side. The other figure was nearer the size of the Viets, but there was something about the way he held his body; he was not an Oriental. Laying the photo down on the coffee table, Rossen got up, went to the kitchen, and came back with a small plastic magnifying glass. It didn't help much. He couldn't make out the faces. The photographer had undoubtedly been in a hurry.

Tomanaga saw the interest on his friend's face. Nodding, pleased, he went into the kitchen to put coffee on. There would be no sleep this night.

It was dawn before the last page was put down. They stared at each other with red, gritty eyes.

"I believe it."

Tomanaga agreed. The evidence was overwhelming. And as Oates had said, the last sighting was two months earlier. It was a better-than-even chance that they'd still be there. If those men had managed to survive the last ten years, then they would probably make it for a while longer.

Rossen poured a shot of whiskey into the bottom of his coffee cup, stirring up the grains which had settled at the bottom. Grimacing, he took a sip.

"We got to do it, Tommy."

"I know."

Rossen took another sip, spitting out dark grains. "I want this one bad. But why doesn't Green show this to the authorities or the press?"

Tomanaga leaned back, rubbing his eyes with the back of his good hand. "Maybe he doesn't want to take a chance on having it

blown. The Viets would just say the pictures
and reports were fakes and deny everything
the way they always do. Or, if it got too hot
for them, they'd just move the POWs to another camp or maybe even kill them if they
got to be too much of an embarrassment."

"You're probably right, Tommy. Okay, let's
put it down for a couple of hours, then we'll
call the Colonel and Green."

Five

They didn't make the call. Green did, jarring them out of a sleep they weren't ready to give up quite yet.

"I'm sorry, fellas, but I had to know. Have you made up your minds yet?"

Grumbling at the receiver, Rossen said, "We'll go for it."

There was a pause on the other end. "I knew you'd do it. Thank you. You won't be sorry."

Rossen snapped back a bit testily. "I al-

ready am if you and the Colonel are going to
spend the rest of your lives waking me and
Tommy up every time we put our heads down."

Relieved laughter came to him over the
phone.

"Okay. You guys go back to sleep. Just remember, we leave this afternoon. I'll call you
in time for you to pack a few things."

The ride from the Denver airport into the
mountains past Gunnison and out to Green's
ranch took several hours. Green led a running
dialogue all the way, detailing one thing or
another. His enthusiasm was infectious and
Tomanaga and Rossen had plenty of questions.

Entering the gate to Green's spread, they
couldn't see much. The ranch sat in a long
narrow valley between peaks reaching up over
ten thousand feet. Nightfall came early.

They were met at the door to a four-thou-
sand-square-foot log cabin by a lean, Levi's-
clad figure carrying an Uzi 9mm submachine
gun.

"Gentlemen, this is Justin. He works with
me and takes care of the place and what guests
I have from time to time. There are others
around, so don't go wandering off unless you
tell me or Justin first."

They weren't surprised that the publisher

had his own security force. His history of rattling cages had made him more than his share of enemies.

Showing them into his living room, he invited them to find a seat while he had a talk with Justin.

Instead of sitting, they wandered around the living room. Plaques, medals, pictures, lined nearly every square inch of the room. On the walls, like at the Colonel's, could be seen Green's history. Among the plaques were a number given to him by officials from El Salvador and Honduras as well as Thailand and several other countries stuck in small corners of the world. Green had been a very busy man since he'd separated from the service.

When he rejoined them, he had another large briefcase with him.

"All right, men, let's get down to facts and see if we can't figure out the best way to bring this thing off."

From the case he removed a large topo map of the area. Like most from that region of the world, it was woefully incomplete with several sections marked NOT CHARTED.

All through that night they went over the maps, making one plan then another, not really expecting to come up with anything viable right out of the chute. This was brain-clearing time, the creative process, when the more unrealistic plans would be eliminated and they would begin to find the bones of what was needed.

Justin played waiter. Not saying much, he brought in fresh pots of coffee, and near dawn came in with a stack of sandwiches which they ate but didn't taste.

For the next three days they spent eighteen and twenty hours at a time going over things. Changing, eliminating, arguing. But bit by bit it began to come together.

Voice raspy from too many cigarettes and lack of sleep, Rossen pointed to the blackboard Green had brought in.

"Okay, let's go over this one more time."

Tomanaga groaned, shaking his head wearily. He was so tired he almost scratched his ass with his claw, forgetting his hook was there for a moment.

"First: We stage out of Thailand. That's obvious; there's no place other than Thailand close enough. Who do we have as a contact there that can be of service and help us get our gear in?

"Second: the gear itself. We know the basics. Weapons, ammo, medical, and chow. How much of each we'll determine later.

"Third: the method of transport to the target area. We only have two choices. By foot or by air. If by air, what do we use? Chopper or plane and where do we get them?

"Fourth: What support can we get from any of the indigenous population? It's going to take more than just Tomanaga and me to get them out, especially if they're sick or too pushed out of shape physically or mentally to help us. We have got to have some help there.

"Fifth: the manner of exfiltration and alternates, remembering there is always the possibility we might have to walk out.

"Bob, you're the one who's going to have to help us on this. So let's go over the items one at a time and you fill us in."

Green stood up, stretching his wiry frame to shake out the knots.

"Right. On items number one and two: Thailand is no problem. I have many friends there who'll give us some help. Also, I can arrange for anything you want in the way of weapons and the rest of your supplies to be there waiting for you, so you don't have to worry about transporting them. That is, of course, unless there are some specialty things I can't get there, but you'll have to fill me in on that later. I can tell you that as long as it's smaller than a tank, I can get it in.

"Item number three: I have, as you already know, done some research on that. I think the best way in is on light aircraft that can hug the mountains and you jump in as close to the target area as possible.

"Item number four: You will have a reception party waiting for you. Mnong tribesmen. They'll be under the command of an old friend of mine. He's the man who obtained the photos for me. He has his own reasons for wanting to help. When we decide on takeoff date, I'll see that he gets the word and you'll be contacted by him or one of his people in Bangkok.

"Item number five: I think it's obvious that the POWs will most likely not be in any shape for a cross-country march through the jungle. We'll pull you all out by air. As you've seen on the maps, there are a number of possible LZs. It will be up to you to select one."

Tomanaga rose to stand beside the publisher. "You know that me and Rossen are specialists. We'll want good ammo, rifles, scopes, and sound suppressors. Can those be obtained in Thailand?"

Green nodded. "No problem. Rossen, you once ran a few shooting courses in Thailand, didn't you?"

"Yeah, but that was a long time ago and I wouldn't trust the equipment anymore. It's too old."

Green had the answers. "You have a contact here who can fix up your weapons the way you want them, don't you?"

"Yeah. There's a couple of other things we'll need to get, too."

Green looked at him questioningly.

"A couple of silencers for .22-caliber automatic pistols. We might need them once we're inside the compound."

Tomanaga agreed. "That would be best. He can do our hand loads for us, too."

Green started to ask the man's name, then thought better of it. They wouldn't tell him, not yet anyway.

Finishing a cup of coffee, Rossen asked Green, "Our man won't do anything bogus. He's got his class-three license to protect, so can you get an end-user certificate for him to Thailand for these things? And once there, are you sure we can get them back?"

Green smiled patiently. "I told you that I can get anything you need in. There's no problem on an end user for Thailand. It's not on the State Department's shit list and I guarantee your order will be waiting for you when you get in-country."

Rossen stood up beside Tommy. "Good enough. If we have no further items to go over at this point, let's call it a night and we'll go see our man tomorrow to firm things up and get a date when he can have everything ready.

*   *   *

They left at dawn in a car loaned to them by Green and were in Colorado Springs in less than three hours.

Tomanaga gave the horn a short push to announce their arrival, then waited in the driveway until the door to the house opened. The man they were coming to see stepped out on his porch wearing, as he had the last time they saw him, the jacket from a set of desert camouflage.

Tomanaga leaned out the window. "Hey, Rich, it's us."

Richard Stroesser's face split into a grin.

"Goddamn. It's good to see you two are still around. I was worried for a while when I didn't hear from you. For a moment or two I thought that you'd finally gotten what you deserved and were no longer in this vale of tears."

They watched him come across the lawn. Lean body, but a feeling to him of inner toughness. Not someone to fuck with. A good man with old-time values.

Opening the door for Tomanaga, he hauled the nisei out to give him a hug as Rossen got out the other door.

"C'mon with me." He led them to the rear of his house where he used his carport as a workshop. Unlocking the door, he ushered them inside.

Directly in front of them was a lathe where he turned barrels; other pieces of machinery were set about between cabinets carrying a paranoid's worst dreams.

The shop wasn't fancy but Stroesser was an artist. He could make anything that came into his hands a bit better, faster, smoother.

On a workbench to the left was one of his .50-caliber sniper's rifles. Rossen went over to it, running a hand over the heavy barrel. Stroesser smiled. "You guys want two more of those?"

"Not this time. We just dropped by to tell you that you're going to get a rush order from the Thai government and thought you might like a little lead time to get things ready."

Stroesser grinned even more broadly. "For the Thai government, huh? And how would you apes know about that?"

Tomanaga reached into one of Stroesser's cabinets, extracting an Uzi with a suppressor on the barrel, working the action appreciatively as Rossen and Stroesser played word games.

"Let's just say a bird shit in our ears. You interested in the order?"

Stroesser bobbed his head up and down. "As long as it's legit, you know that. Now, what is it?"

Wiping small steel filings from a metal table, Rossen set his hip on it.

"First, they'll want two of your Rugers, the ones you make with the extended barrels and integral suppressors. Also, two laser sights for each."

Stroesser nodded. "What else?"

"They also want two M-14s, and they want them completely gone over. Glass-embedded stocks, the actions reworked, everything. Also, two of those scopes you sold to us last time. You know, the Shephard scope; and two of the new Starlight devices. They'll also need five hundred rounds of 7.62 ammo for the M-14s. I think they'd like the same kind of loads me and Tommy use."

Stroesser went to a cabinet, taking out a tape measure.

"I presume the Thai gentlemen who will be firing these pieces are the same size as you and Tomanaga?"

Rossen looked a bit sheepish as Stroesser measured him, taking down the distances exact to a millimeter. When he was finished, the rifle would have the precise length of the distance from Rossen's shoulder to his trigger finger. Then he took another measurement to determine the best position for the scope mounts so the best possible eye relief would be built into the system. Pushing Rossen out of the way when he was finished, he did Tomanaga, commenting dryly to him as he did so: "You know, the odds on fitting out a rifle for another man thousands of miles away that you've never seen who is also your exact size and has a hook for a trigger finger must be incredible."

Tomanaga agreed. "Yes, it is truly fantastic, but the ways of the gods and fate are supposed to be inscrutable, aren't they?"

When they finished, Tomanaga went back inside the cabinet and came up with two scabbards. "You want one of these, Sam?" He tossed one of the weapons over to him.

The blade looked like a miniature Samurai sword, surprisingly heavy with molded etched rubber grips. Tanto blades. Tomanaga knew what he was talking about. The angle of the slicing edge was designed to give maximum depth on a slice and the point was still good for a straight thrust. A lot better than the current craze for double-edged daggers, which weren't worth a shit for cutting, Rossen thought. "Yeah. I'd like one, too."

Stroesser waved his hand magnanimously. "Keep them as parting gifts. I got a feeling that you guys aren't going to be around here too long."

"The date when you can have the order ready, Rich, we need to know that."

"Wait a minute." Stroesser went over to his desk, thumbed a well-worn address book, dialed a number, talked for a minute, and turned back to them. "I can have the rifles here in two days. It'll take me another four to redo them and a couple more to make up the ammo; then I want to test-fire them on the range. We're looking at eight days max. That okay?"

Rossen put the Tanto blade into a rear pocket. "That'll work out fine, but me and Tomanaga will come in for the testing. I want to get the feel of them myself before recommending them to our friends."

Stroesser gave a lopsided sardonic grin, still playing the game. "Naturally. Why am I not surprised?"

He returned to his workshop, his mind already going ahead to the job of taking the two national match rifles and reworking them. There was a lot to be done besides the obvious things Rossen had requested:

He was going to drill and tap the side of the receiver and install a dovetail base, then adapt the scope mount to accommodate the dovetail.

Replace the issue barrel with a Douglass air-gauged barrel (which would guarantee consistency in tolerances throughout the length of the barrel to within one tenth of a thousandth inch; the rifling is hand-lapped, which gets rid of all the chatter marks normally found in most commercial rifle barrels).

Fit a new gas piston. Extra trigger guard group in case there was malfunction in the field.

Change the system so the flash break could be unthreaded, and the suppressor put on the barrel directly, giving it better alignment. It also would make the mount stronger, giving it more strength in case it was jarred or bumped.

As for the ammo, he'd also make up a hundred rounds using a 193-grain boattail bullet to give the best ballistic coefficiency for distance shooting, and a full-jacketed round with a core of fulminate of mercury.

——————————————— Six

Green didn't bat an eye at the price. Rossen felt that if they had ordered a tank or two it wouldn't have mattered. This was not a matter of money and Green meant what he had said. He would spend every dime he had to get out just one MIA.

Taking the list, he retired to his office; in half an hour he came back, returning the list to them.

"The order and the end-user certificate will

be in the mail to your friend tomorrow, along
with full payment."

"Good enough." Rossen moved toward the
door. " 'Till he has it ready, me and Tomanaga
are going to head up in the hills to get our
wind and legs back. A few days backpacking
will do us good. We've been cooped up here
long enough."

Green agreed. "You're right. Just don't fall
off a mountain and make sure you come back
a couple of days before the weapons are ready
in case anything new comes up that we need
to talk over. By the time you're back, I'll have
your visas and tickets ready."

They pulled out at dawn the next morning.
Green's backyard rested on the base of a series of mountains and valleys that run for
hundreds of miles. Plenty of room to get lost
in. Justin took them to the property line in a
jeep and let them off.

Tomanaga took the point, following a deer
trail which would take them up into the highlands near treeline where the air was crisp
and cool.

Both of them needed this time away. No
guns. No noise or people. Time to try and sort
themselves out, to prepare mentally for what
was coming. Neither had any illusions about
the job going down easy. Before it was over,
men were going to die and they might be

among them. Death was something which didn't frighten them—they had been too close to it too many times to be afraid of it. Only the manner of death was of any importance. That one day they would die mattered only in who the survivor was going to be. Each hoped that it would not be he.

On trips like these, when they were alone, they tried to find the reasons which made them what they were and each time they failed. Once Rossen had even suggested trying to find the shrink from Vietnam, what's his name, Asher. Yeah, that was it. Dr. Sidney Asher. Once or twice Rossen had felt during their interviews that the small quick man had come very close to touching something in him that might have given him answers, then backed away, afraid of what they might be.

Asher had once told him the biggest problem with psychiatrists and analysts is when they begin to question everything they do, looking for underlying causes and motives. After a time it makes them crazy.

As he had a thousand times before, Rossen watched the back of the nisei breaking ground in front of him. It had taken a long time for them to become friends. He hadn't known how. But once he had let his shield down long enough for Tomanaga to get inside, he had never been lonely again. He had a friend, and

Tomanaga had softened him in a good way.
Tommy had a quiet easy strength and sense
of humor to him that made him—Rossen—the
stronger for having him as a friend.

While they were gone the rest of the job
went on. Green opened his lines of commmu-
nication with his contacts in Thailand, pre-
paring the ground for Tomanaga and Rossen.
Stroesser was hard at work in his small shop,
filling their order. Not even waiting for the
rifles to come in, he started on the ammo the
same day the order had been placed. Each
round was prepared with loving care: A fail-
ure on any part of his job could result in the
death of men he liked.

By the time they returned from the mountain, smelling of woodsmoke and sweat, Green
was ready for them. Their papers were in;
only shots were needed. He took care of that
by taking them to his own doctor. Everything
was brought up to date. Tetanus, typhoid, chol-
era, plague, and gamma globulin for hepatitis.
They'd start on antimalarial drugs the day
they hit country.

No new data had come in, and though they
went over their basic plan half a dozen times
more, there was nothing they could add to it.

Any other changes would have to come once they were on-site.

Tomanaga called Stroesser on the morning of the seventh day.

"Hey, Tommy. I think you guys should come on down and visit me for a day. Your friends' order is ready."

Passing the info on to Rossen, he received the nod. "Right you are, Rich. We'll see you about noon tomorrow, okay?"

"Okay, little buddy. I'll stay at home till I hear from you."

"Good enough. Take care. Hear?"

Green was trembling with excitement; the hours had grown small. "Good. Very good. If everything's all right, then I want you two on a plane the next day, okay?"

Rossen patted him on the shoulder. "Yeah. That's all right. We got nothing else to do here, so we might as well get on with the show."

As before, Tomanaga took the wheel. He liked to drive better than Rossen did. Leaning back in the seat, Rossen closed his eyes to let the miles roll past. Letting his mind go. He wished they were able to take at least one of the .50-caliber sniper's rifles with them. It was a hell of a weapon. Before they had taken on the last job they had done one other piece of work for Juliano and Popo, the Deputy Comandante. For that they had arranged for two of Stroesser's heavy rifles. Being bolt action, they didn't come under any weapons restriction. Anyone could buy them if they had the price. Juliano had gotten his hands on two of them after being told of them by Rossen. They fit exactly into some plans the former Sandinista pilot had for his onetime compatriots.

Tomanaga took his eyes off the road for a moment looking over at Rossen's sleeping face. He knew he was dreaming by the way his eyes jerked back and forth under their lids.

Pushing back against his shoulder, the recoil was surprisingly small. He'd thought that with a weapon firing a .50-cal slug the recoil would have been much worse. Actually it was less than that of a 7.62mm. It was more of a firm shove than a kick. Not too uncomfortable at all.

As with the last five rounds, all had hit the targets on the field below. It was incredible: At ranges of fifteen to nineteen hundred meters he was having no problem keeping a respectable shot grouping.

Tomanaga had some problems at first, until the stock was modified to accept his claw. Once that problem was resolved, he, too, was making good hits.

On the field below was a layout of an airstrip with targets set at the right distances for fuel trucks, storage tanks, aircraft, and a large tree that served as the tower, a piece of white board nailed to it representing the doorway at the base. For the last three days they had been on the range constantly, firing in all manners of light from pitch-black to noonday. This was the last day. They knew their weapons, they knew their targets.

"How's it going, compadres? Will they do the job?"

"I do believe they will, Juliano. These two things are going to be a hell of a surprise."

He and Tomanaga picked up the two .50-cal sniper's rifles. Their weight was close to that of one of the old Browning automatic rifles: twenty-two pounds. A bit heavy for any fast-track work but one hell of a steady firing platform.

Walking to their Land-Rover, they put the rifles in the back, covering them with a blanket. Tomanaga climbed into the back seat, letting Rossen sit up front so he could talk to Juliano.

Leaving their makeshift range, they headed for the *finca* of Don Luis, one of the Costa Ricans who supported the Contra movement. It was on his farm that they had set up their range. It had a small wooded ridge similar to that of the real target. That had been important; they needed to know everything about the characteristics of the weapon to be able to compensate for shooting fifteen degrees downhill and be able to figure the proper minutes of drop for each piece with different rounds. Their best—or at least their most consistent—groups came from using the AIP rounds.

Rossen and Juliano talked over the operation, settling last-minute differences and questions. They would go in the next night just at dusk using one of the two operational Loaches the Contras had in service. They would be dropped off three kilometers from the target area with a backup crew to help them with the weapons, carry the ammo, and provide security for the operation while they did their number. The chopper would stay on the deck until they returned or were an hour late. He and Tommy fully intended to be on time. The thought of trying to bug out on foot through miles of Indian country didn't appeal very much to them.

At Don Luis's, Juliano put the jeep into the woods behind the house, just in case the Costa Ricans came snooping around. Lately they had been coming down a bit hard on the Contras, especially since there had been a couple of minor altercations with the Sandinistas on their border. Shots had been fired. A couple of mortar rounds had landed on their side of the border. The Costa Rican government was desperately trying to stay neutral. Not an easy thing to do but they tried, and part of that effort included making occasional half-hearted sweeps in areas known to support the guerrillas.

They did this without being too hard on the Contras; the guerrilla force in their area was larger than their own *guardia* and much better armed. For their part the Contras ordered their men not to fire on the Costa Ricans even if they were arrested. So far so good and no one had been hurt. But you never knew when that would change. All it took was for one man on either side to get a bit nervous and the killing could start. That was something both sides wanted to avoid like the plague.

The insertion was done the usual way, with one of their old Loach helicopters. Juliano took them in, a smile on his face, confident as he maneuvered near treetop level over valleys and across rivers. They had finally gotten an artificial horizon for the chopper. To the west, banks of clouds were rolling in from the warm waters of the Caribbean; it would rain somewhere around sundown, the time when they were due to hit the deck.

Rossen sat in front with Juliano; Tomanaga was in the back with Roberto and Negron. They had also worked together before. Ro-

berto and Negron were the first two men he
and Tomanaga trained when they had taken
their first job with the Contras. Both were
tough, wiry men nearly fifty years old but
who could move like mountain goats. Small,
strong men whose stern Indian faces could
break into bright smiles easily. Good men.
They kept things basic.

The rear compartment had no seats; you
just found a place, squatted down, and hung
on. The only thing strapped in were the two
.50-cal rifles. The passengers just took their
chances.

Beneath, the earth was green. Ten thousand
shades of green. From the air nothing could
be seen beneath the canopy of trees. Only
when they passed over small patches of fire-
cleared jungle where small family groups of
Indians, most of them refugees, planted their
corn and plantains was anything but cover
visible.

Juliano spoke to Rossen over the intercom.
"We're in Sandino land now. Keep your eyes
open."

Leaning back to where he could turn his
head and see Tomanaga, he passed it on. "Keep
a lookout, Tommy. Juliano says this is Indian
country."

Tomanaga turned to face out the open hatch;
Roberto took the other side. Tommy had

Negron's M-14. They were no match for the heavily armed Hip-8 or Mi-24s, but it made them feel a bit better. In a chase, the old Loach would leave the Russian battle choppers standing still. It was faster and more maneuverable and that was its main and only real defense.

Behind them, the shadows were growing longer. By the time Juliano let them off and headed back, it would be full dark. He didn't like flying at night in the worn-out old bird but for this job it had to be done.

"We're going down," he informed Rossen. Banking to the port, he skimmed over the tops of a group of trees, down a small valley, then pulled up and took a look to orient himself. They headed north a couple of hundred yards to hover over a clearing in the jungle not seventy feet across. The Loach settled on the earth in a cloud of leaves and detritus.

They bailed out in a hurry, hauling the heavy rifles out and away from the blades of the chopper. Juliano wasted no time. As soon as his passengers were in the clear he was back up and moving. He would take a zigzag course for a time before heading back to the south, so if anyone did have a fix on him it would be hard for them to pinpoint where he had made his drop-off.

After the steady drone of the chopper blades

in their ears, then the rushing roar as it took off, the sound of silence was deafening, eerie. The jungle was quiet now, the animals frightened into silence by the metal bird. It didn't last long. Within seconds the first chirps, croaks, and trills of birds began to reestablish themselves, proclaiming their hunting areas.

Roberto and Negron each hefted one of the heavy rifles to their shoulders. Rossen and Tomanaga took the M-14s. There was no argument from their willing porters. The dour-faced Indians knew who the best shots were. Taking a compass sight, Rossen led off, Roberto and Negron in the middle and Tomanaga bringing up drag. They still had ten clicks to go this night before they would be able to set their loads down. Those ten kilometers would take them ten hours. It would be around 0400 before they reached their target area and set up for the predawn's work. Then they would have to move out and return the way they had come in order to meet the pickup. All in all, it was going to be a ball-busting job any way you looked at it.

With sunfall Rossen took to using the Starlight scope on the M-14. After taking a compass reading, he would sight the scope on an object as far as he could see and use it for a checkpoint. When he reached it, he would repeat the process. This way they stayed fairly close to their course. There was no talking. Only the sound of lungs sucking in air between teeth was to be heard from them. The rest of the night sounds belonged to the wild-life, the monkeys and birds. From behind, Roberto would touch Rossen's arm from time to time, indicating where they would have to go when they came to a split on the narrow animal trail they had followed from the LZ. He and Negron had twice made the trip during the last month. They didn't need the compass and Starlight to know which way to go. But if it made the big gringo happier to use them, then they had no argument. Either way they would be on time and at the right place.

Minutes after they had set down, sweat had begun to ooze out of open pores. There was no breeze—only still, weighted air that clogged the nostrils and set heavy in the lungs. At the halfway mark Roberto indicated they could take a break.

Setting their loads down, all of them opened their tunics to let the skin breathe. Resting his back against a tree, Tomanaga looked up into the night sky. Peering between the few breaks in the overhead cover, he could see the moon rising to the center of the night. Bright, silver, clear, it looked cool, peaceful. From the few beams it was able to cast to the jungle floor he could make out the figures of Rossen and the others, the sweat on their faces and chests gleaming like tiny crystals. There was still no talking.

Tomanaga's stump ached. But then it always ached. He wished he could take the hook off and rub it but this was not the time.

Opening his canteen, he took a long pull and passed it around to the others. They would all use the same canteen and drink till it was empty. There would be no small gurgling sound coming from a half-filled canteen to give them away. It was the small things that got you killed most often. When you broke the rules you paid for it eventually.

He and Rossen had only managed to live this long by staying to the game plan and making those around them do the same. Rossen had even made Juliano find them some camouflage BDVs made in Argentina which were 100 percent cotton. Fatigues with a synthetic fiber used in them whispered when the material rubbed together.

Several times he and Tomanaga had offered to take over the carrying of the .50s but neither Roberto nor Negron would hear of it. That was their job. The gringos must not be too tired. Exhaustion could make the hand tremble, causing a shot to miss. This was too important. They would carry the load all the way.

Twice more they took breaks till Roberto again touched Rossen's arm. Placing a finger to his eye, he pointed to the north where a fork in the trail led into dense bush.

"Periquackos," he hissed, the first and last word that was spoken.

This was the split. From their briefing they knew there was a Sandinista outpost a few hundred meters down the trail to the right. This was the place to switch loads. Giving Roberto and Negron the rifles, he and Tommy took the heavy .50s and the ammo. Roberto and Negron would go down the right-hand trail. Their job would be to take out the Sandinistas at the outpost, then return to give them cover.

Silently, they shook hands, gave each other an *abrazo*, and split up. He and Tomanaga headed to the left. The time was 0415. They were a few minutes behind schedule but not enough to matter. The killing season wouldn't open till just before sunrise. Humping it up a long rise for another ten minutes, they came to the site. Setting their loads down, they lay on their bellies to scope out the target. There it was! A new chopper pad cut out of the jungle. This was to be a forward base for the Russian-made, and usually Cuban-flown, assault helicopters. Around the base the jungle had been cut back to a max of five hundred meters; the entire area was heavily mined and booby-trapped. Four aprons of barbed wire and concertina surrounded the entire complex.

At regular intervals of one hundred meters on the inner apron were machine-gun bunkers with lesser positions interspersed between them. Two high guard towers with searchlights swept the cleared ground constantly. Inside the compound were several heavy mortar pits and additional bunkers set in an apron surrounding the barracks and headquarters. To the east was what Rossen wanted. Seven helicopters. Hip-8s and Mi-24s placed in sandbagged cubicles. Only from a high placement such as the one he and Tomanaga were on could the bodies of the helicopters be seen. Just north of the choppers were three fuel tankers filled with gas. Twenty meters beyond them were static tanks half buried in the ground, also filled with fuel. Flashlights from walking sentries could be easily seen. Even at this hour the chopper strip was on constant alert.

From the briefing Juliano had given them, they knew there were at least five hundred troops down there, two hundred of them Cubans, most of them veterans from Ethiopia and Angola. For the Contras to have tried a conventional attack would have been suicide. Not twenty minutes away were the jet fighters and bombers at the field outside of Managua. It would have been a slaughter. But maybe he and Tomanaga could do the thing for them in less time with no casualties. Hopefully.

Taking their time, they set up their weapons, putting on the Shephard scopes with the special grid built into them for long-distance shooting. Rossen tried to adjust the bipod legs and took a sighting on the field. He didn't like the feel and took the bipods off, letting the barrel of the rifle rest on his pack. He took another sight and was satisfied.

Tomanaga moved a few feet away from him and took up his position. He kept the bipod legs on. Each of them set out rounds for their rifles, removed the bolt, and put in one shell, chambering the round and locking it down. Once this was done they moved about to bring in more cover and camouflage their positions. After that there was nothing to do but wait. The time was 0520 hours.

From where they were the sun would come up behind them and be in the eyes of the defenders; that should help to cover a bit of their weapons' muzzle flashes. If things went as planned, they shouldn't be on-site more than ten minutes after the first round was fired. At that moment Roberto and Negron would take out the outpost and move to rejoin them. Ten minutes, not very long.

Dawn came inching at first, then picking up speed. The first light seeping through a bank of clouds turned the morning sky to the east the color of blood mixed with rainbows. It was nearly time. They took their canteens and watered down the ground in front and to the sides of their rifles to keep dust from being thrown up in the blast from the muzzle brake.

It was time, they had settled on their targets. Raising the butt plates of the .50s to their shoulders, they settled in.

Through the scopes there was more than enough light to make out the shapes of their targets resting in their private bunkers. Rossen would take the first shot, then Tomanaga would come in. With the short bolt action of the rifles they knew they could put out a max of ten effective rounds a minute between them.

Taking a breath, Rossen set the range on the lines for fifteen hundred meters. A kilometer and a half.

As always this was the time when one had to let the mind go. Let the body and reflexes take over. All responses were autonomic, one simply became part of the weapon, a device to serve the needs of the heavy gun.

The first round was out of the chamber before he knew his finger had taken up the last thousandths of a pound of pressure. Heavy, the rifle shoved back against his shoulder.

Through the expanded image of the scope he watched the first shot take effect.

Seven hundred and fifty grains, tungsten-carbide core traveling at 2,700 feet per second. At a hundred yards the armor-piercing incendiary could penetrate two inches of homogenous steel; at a thousand yards a half inch of the same steel. The tank wall of the fuel truck presented no difficulty.

He kept his eye on the target to make certain his first round was where it was supposed to be and the sight didn't need any adjustment. The truck exploded, erupting in a blazing mass of black smoke and red spreading flames. Burning gasoline sprayed out for a hundred meters in all directions. The explosion covered Tomanaga's shot, which took out the second truck, gas spreading out on the earth.

The Sandinos reacted in confusion. From the barracks troops poured forth. Searchlights swept the area. There was no fire coming from the chopper base to the outside.

Good. They probably thought the explosions were caused by sabotage. Rossen chambered another round.

His next shot hit the fuel tank on one of the Hip-8s. It didn't explode, just began to burn slowly in its sandbagged enclosure. Tomanaga stayed on the fuel targets, sending rounds into the dug-in fuel tanks. It took four to get them started, but when they went, the roar of the explosion sent shock waves reaching to the hills, as men were knocked from their feet and vehicles tossed like children's toys. Men began to burn, too, as fiery rain fell from the skys to land on the clothing and skin of running figures. A machine-gun bunker disappeared in a raining furnace as hundreds of gallons of burning fuel fell from the sky to cover the explosion. Inside, men were shriveled to charred stick figures as the ammo in the bunker began to explode. The Sandinos took cover; no one ventured out if they could take shelter.

Rossen took another shot, this time taking out an Mi-24 as its pilot attempted to get the machine airborne and out of the furnace. Knowing where to place the shot—that was the trick. Even at fifteen hundred meters he could get a good shot group. His round exploded the Plexiglas windshield. The heavy slug just clipped the tip of the pilot's shoulder, but the impact was such that the shock waves from the bullet caused multiple fractures down to his elbow. The chopper wavered as the pilot lost control; rose to about fifty feet then slipped to the side to land on a field of flame and burn quietly until its own tanks caught fire and the machine-gun and rocket ammo on board exploded.

The Sandinos still didn't know what the score was. Now the explosions inside their own compound were covering the selective shots fired from the hillside a kilometer and a half away.

They turned their attention to the choppers full-time. With the .50s there was no way to rush anything; it demanded they take their time. Each shot was carefully placed; if they couldn't set the chopper on fire, they concentrated on the hump on the chopper back where the turbine and rotor system was most fragile. At least the bird would be out of action for a long time. Rossen didn't notice the ache from the recoil shove of the heavy rifle; his shoulder had grown numb.

In panic the defenders below began to fire at random all around the base. None of the return fire came even remotely close to their position. Five minutes had passed. On the field below, five helicopters were burning, another three damaged. Now it was time to begin to break contact. They had done enough. Seeping fuel from one of the ruptured tanks flowed into one of the mortar pits. The earth shook, trembling as the rounds for the tube exploded, some being thrown over a hundred feet into the air to explode, raining down burning shrapnel. Several of them were white-phosphorus rounds; they added to the fires spreading over the camp. The HQ and barracks were beginning to burn.

They pulled back out of sight and started down the trail, hauling their weapons with them. As they did, they missed seeing one of the Hind helicopters get airborne. Its crew of Cubans had managed to get it up and it was fully loaded. Accidentally, they headed in the direction of the sniping party.

Swooping over the outpost where Roberto and Negron had killed the six occupants as soon as the firing started, the pilot could see the dead lying about. Pulling up for a bit more altitude, he could make out a thin trail running beneath the trees. He followed it.

Roberto and Negron waved to Rossen and Tomanaga urging them to hurry up. Rossen kept his .50, running with the weapon cradled in his arms, vapor still rising from the oiled breech. Tomanaga stumbled and Roberto grabbed him, hauling him back to his feet as Negron picked up the fallen rifle and took off after Rossen.

A rushing noise swept over them at the same time as the shadow of the Hind. Negron disappeared. He simply wasn't there anymore. He had caught the full burst from the 12.7mm machine gun in the nose of the Mi-24. It had blown him to pieces, scattering his parts over the trail. Tomanaga stumbled through the bloody mist of what had been Negron.

There was no time to stand and fight or even use the remaining .50 against the hump-backed armored helicopter. All they could do now was try to break contact. The weight of the .50 was dragging Rossen down. Cursing, he set it on the trail, removed a thermite grenade from his webbing, and set it on the gun's breech after opening the bolt.

They were long gone by the time the dull thump and cloud of smoke told him the weapon had been destroyed. Too bad. It was a good piece, but it had served its purpose, and now they had to take care of their own asses before the Hind ate their cake for them. Then, suddenly, there was quiet; the chopper was gone. The commander had received a panic-laden call to return to the field and give the defenders support against the ground assault which the field commander was certain was to come in the next seconds. They were let off the hook.

When they reached the LZ, Juliano was there waiting. He said nothing when he saw the expressions on their faces. Negron was gone, but the field had been hit and hit hard. It would be some time before the Sandinistas would be able to replace their losses, and from

now on they would never feel 100 percent
secure. A new lesson had been learned by all
concerned: At the cost of two rifles and one
man they had destroyed millions of dollars of
equipment. As for the number of enemy dead,
that was open to conjecture.

Juliano lifted them up into the sky.

They were taken out.

Rossen's eyes jerked open as the car came
to a sudden stop at a red light. He was back.

Seven

One day on the range proved that Stroesser had once more done an outstanding job. Everything tested out to perfection. By the time they left to return to the ranch, he had already packed up the weapons, ammo, and sights for shipment to the end user. They would go directly to the Thai embassy in Washington, D.C., then be sent by diplomatic pouch to Bangkok.

When they got back to the ranch, Green was more antsy than they were.

"You are ready to go, aren't you? I've got everything ready. There's a flight out of Denver at midnight."

Tomanaga would have laughed except Green was stone serious. He wanted them on the way.

Rossen answered for them both.

"Why not? We can sleep on the plane."

"Good, good!" Green ejaculated. "Here are your tickets and visas along with press credentials from my company. I checked with the embassy; everything's in order."

Handing over a slip of paper, he added, "Call this number when you get in and you'll be met when you get to the hotel. A friend of mine will call and identify himself. You met him once before so it won't be too much of a surprise."

Hustling them out the door to the waiting car, he kept on his running monologue, not giving them a chance to speak as if afraid that at the last minute they might ask him something that he couldn't answer and they would call off the job.

From Manila they traveled on Garuda, the Thai national airline. A sense of déjà vu rushed over both of them. This was the first time they had been back to Southeast Asia since the end of the Vietnam War. In many ways it was in Vietnam that their lives had really begun. There in the cesspool of corruption, mismanagement, and blood they had become the men they were today and there was no retreat from that, ever.

Touching down, they cleared customs, standing in a line of thirty Japanese on holiday to test and sample the fleshpots for which Thailand was world-famous. The customs officer gave them only a cursory examination as he went through their bags, stamped the tags on them, and waved them through to the outside where the heat and smell of Asia washed over them. No place on the face of the earth has the same texture to it as Asia. Rich, ripe, almost to the point of sweet nausea, the texture of the air clung to the back of the palate and throat, nearly choking them. That would pass, and soon the smells and heaviness of the air would seem normal.

A three-year-old Mercedes taxi took them to the Rajah hotel on Soi Nana North. Rossen didn't like it. Its clientele was mostly European, and a bit strange for his taste. It was later that he found out it was the only hotel listed in the tour guide that was not recommended for families. He would have been happier if they'd been checked into one of the local hotels. But the man paying the bills had set the trip up.

Once they were checked into their rooms, Rossen waded through the scraps of paper in his billfold until he found the number he wanted. Green was right; he did know the man. Or at least once long ago he had known Colonel Ramasavet. Now he headed one of Thailand's many security services. Just what he actually did they didn't know, but during the war Rossen had trained him and several other Thai officers in quick-kill techniques. He, Tomanaga, and Rossen had become, if not asshole buddies, at least friendly.

Ram had told them once that what he had learned from them saved his life more than once, and if he could ever be of service to them he would be most honored to do so. That was what they were banking on now: that Ram would come across with some support from the military and maybe some updated input on the MIA situation, or at least some current information as to the dispositions of enemy forces in the target area.

Tomanaga removed his claw, massaging the reddened stump. It had been sore for the last few days. The only reason he had worn the prosthesis through customs was so he wouldn't have to answer dumb questions about what the hook was for. Not all customs officials are among the brightest people in the world. Anything out of the norm could send them into a state of mental diarrhea.

"Hey, Rossen. I'm going to take a shower and soak this thing. Okay?"

"Yeah, go ahead. I'll try to reach Ram."

It took nearly half an hour before he got connected with an office where he finally found someone who spoke English and patched him through to Ram's office. Rossen still didn't know what section he was with. After giving his name seven or eight times he was finally greeted by a girlish, high-pitched voice.

"Hey, Shooter. Is that you?"

Ram spoke excellent English, having attended many of those fine service schools the American Armed Forces make available to foreign officers.

"Yeah, it's me, Ram. How the hell are you? It's been a long time."

On the other end was a pause as Ram collected his thoughts.

"Shooter, I know that you are not here on vacation, but this is not the time to talk. You have called me because of our mutual friend and also perhaps to keep a promise I once made. Let me assure you that the promise still stands. I keep my word. When do you wish to meet?"

"As soon as possible, Ram, we're at the—"

Ram cut him off. "I know where you are.

Stay there; I will be over in a couple of hours. By the way, tell your old backup man that I send him my regards."

"Yes, he's here with me. We'll be waiting."

"Very good, Shooter. I will be over as I said, within two hours. Please be there and make no further calls or contacts with anyone in the city till after we have talked."

Hanging up the receiver, Rossen shook his head. Ramasavet was a smart little shit. If he was on their side, it could simplify a lot of things. He wondered how Green had gotten to him. One thing he knew about Ram was that he was not cheap. All of a sudden the deal was looking better; in fact, not bad at all, and it told him a lot. Green carried some pretty heavy-duty clout.

Tomanaga came out of the shower wearing a hakata, the short-style Japanese cotton robe, and lay down on his bed near the air conditioner.

Rossen warned him. "Remember Honduras when we checked into the Holiday Inn there because they had hot water and air-conditioning? You caught pneumonia. So watch it! Neither of us can afford to get sick now." Grudgingly, Tomanaga turned the air conditioner down to low and pulled the bedcover over him.

"Did you reach Ram?"

"Uh-huh, he's coming over in a couple of hours. He asked about you, too. I think that he's going to be helpful. But we'll just have to wait and see."

Colonel Ramasavet Bandurapanthe of the Thai Royal Security Service was a man of many responsibilities and parts. Often he amused himself by thinking of his life as that of a golden spider who spun webs of silver throughout the country and even into neighboring states. Silver threads that pieces of information and often people became stuck to. When he felt the tremble of the thread which signaled that someone or something had touched his web, he would slowly, carefully draw the thread in. Then he would examine his catch. Some he would cover over to use later and some he would eat then, digesting everything, leaving only hollow husks as evidence of their passage.

Now he was on his way to test another thread. This one he had to be careful with. The Shooter was a different kind of catch. How or if he could be used to his advantage was still to be determined. His mission in Thailand was of interest but all the ramifications were as of this moment unclear. But that would pass, as did the eternal mists which rested over the golden-domed wats of Krung Thep.

Personally, he liked the big American and his partner. Several times in the past few years he had heard rumors of them and what they had been doing. He was not surprised. For men like them there were few choices. They had long since become infected, an infection which was always terminal. The date of termination was the matter which was not known. It might come with the next heartbeat.

He had driven himself to the hotel wearing civilian dress as to not attract undue attention. He handed the car over to a porter and entered the lobby of one of the more decadent facilities his city had to offer.

Going straight to the elevator, he made mental notes of everyone he saw in the lobby; several were men he knew of but had not met. Smugglers, buyers for the opium of the Gold Triangle, and journalists mixed in about equal proportion with tourists in ugly shirts and hairy legs. Most unpleasant.

Knocking on the door, he announced himself. "It is I. I believe we have an appointment."

Opening the door, Rossen showed him in. Their initial greeting was formal, proper. Ramasavet was not one who let people get very close to him. You knew instinctively that he did not like being touched. For him to offer

to shake hands first was a major sign of good-
will. Rossen took Ram's girlish hand in his
larger paw.

"Good to see you, sir. It has been a long
time."

Ram nodded in agreement. "Yes, the years
have gone by very swiftly. But it seems as
though the world has learned nothing. It still
bleeds, cries, and starves when none of that is
necessary. May I sit?"

"Of course, Colonel." Rossen indicated the
couch. Settling his lean body comfortably down
on the polyester cushions, he looked over at
Tomanaga, who was just waking up.

"Greetings, Tomanaga-san. Welcome back."

Tomanaga started to rub the sleep out of
his eye with his left hand when he remembered that he didn't have one and switched.

"Hello, Ram. You look pretty good for an
old man."

"Thank you. Kind words are always appre-
ciated. May I say the same for you, save that
you appear a bit weary."

Tomanaga sat up, the sheet dropping off his
upper torso, revealing a body that could have
been crafted by the chisel of a master sculp-
tor. Not an ounce of fat or sag showed. When
he moved, wiry bands of muscle twitched under his skin, writhing and turning. Tomanaga
had taken care of himself. Ram sighed a bit

with self-recrimination at the slight paunch he had started to develop.

Rossen moved a chair over to where he could face Ram and see his eyes.

"We need your help." Ram waited for him to continue, saying nothing.

Rossen cleared his throat. "Look, I know that recently there have been a number of squirrels here for basically the same reason and they have fucked things up pretty good. But I think you know that me and Tomanaga work differently."

Ram still made no comment, only nodding his head for Rossen to continue.

Tomanaga had gotten out of bed and put on his trousers, then stood beside Rossen.

"As I am sure Green told you, we're here to try and bring out an MIA."

Ram responded for the first time. "What makes you think you can succeed where the others have failed?"

Rossen and Tomanaga noted that Ram did not make any observation as to why they believed there were any MIAs still alive. That was significant.

"Because we have had a hard sighting and photo. Our employer, as you know, has a lot of bucks and many contacts. We know there is at least one MIA alive at a camp on the Laotian border near where Cambodia and Vietnam join. This is no bullshit. The man was there as of two months ago."

Ram shook out a cigarette from a pack of American Salems and lit up, drawing the menthol-laden smoke deep into his lungs, then letting it out slowly before saying quietly, "First, understand that I am on your side in this matter. In my mind there is no doubt that Americans are still being held by the communists. They have done it before, you know. After the French were kicked out they held on to several thousand prisoners for over seven years, releasing them only when a form of blackmail was paid by the French government. As to their response about retaining prisoners of war, they claimed the men they kept behind were not entitled to such treatment or consideration. They were not POWs. Instead, they were ordinary criminals who had been sentenced lawfully by their courts.

"A thin excuse, but it served their purpose. Perhaps that is what they are doing with your men. Holding them till reparations are made. I do not know for certain and can only speculate."

Rossen had heard that story before, and knew it was true. He had once met one of the French legionnaires who had been kept captive by the Viet Minh for six years after the war was over.

Ram took another long pull at the Salem and butted it. "What do you wish of me?"

It was 'fess-up time. If they were to be able to do any more, they had to level with Ram and get his assistance.

"We need what dope you can give on the current situation in Laos and Vietnam. We need transport, if it can be had, to take us in as close as possible. If we try to cross that jungle on foot it could take a couple of months and we'd probably never make it. We need a lot of help, but if we can get in, you have known us long enough to know that we can do the job. Once we're on-site, if there is an MIA alive in the camp, we'll get him back out."

There were a few men who could make such a statement and have Ram believe them. These were two of them. He knew the capabilities of the Shooter and the Japanese. Once they were committed, there would be no stopping them short of death, and they had proven to be very difficult to kill.

Ram stood. "This is a very touchy matter. I will have to make some calls and talk to a few people. Also, I will see that the other man Mr. Green spoke of presents himself shortly.

"However, believe me when I say that most of the people in my government are in sympathy with you and we certainly have no liking for the communists. If it is possible to discredit them in the eyes of the world, it could be of value to us in the troubles we have with them at the border. I will do what I can and get back to you. Until then, please do not speak to anyone of this matter or attempt to go any further on your own. Stay close to the hotel, as I may need to get hold of you instantly."

He went to the door, opening it. Before leaving, he turned, once more stated firmly, "Talk to no one else. If you do, then I would have no choice but to have you arrested and deported. This must not become public knowledge. Remember I am on your side in this matter."

The door closed, leaving Rossen and Tomanaga alone. Once more it was sit-on-your-fucking-thumbs time, waiting for someone else to deliver. They might have had more confidence in Ram if they had known that he had already been on the job for two months. A colonel's pay in Thailand is less than extravagant, and the fifteen thousand American dollar advance the publisher had given would go a long way toward ensuring his comfortable retirement. Still, Ram had the satisfaction of knowing that he was not doing it for the money alone. He was in sympathy with the two snipers and so was his government. What the politicians were afraid of was another botched job. These two were different. He would give them what they needed, but first he had to contact the publisher for more money. There were going to be some additional expenses.

Eight

From his office Ramasavet began to pull his strings, tugging one gently here, giving the next a firm jerk, sending out ripples and waves to those at the ends of his web. Then he, too, had to wait for responses, though they were not long in coming. In two days he had all he needed to know, but waited another three before calling Rossen and Tomanaga. It was always best not to make what he had done appear too simple. Simple solutions cost little; difficulties paid more.

However, it was now time to have another chat with the shooters. Seng Pouk, the leader of a small band of Mnong rebels, would arrive in Bangkok this very evening. Then the plan could shift into high gear, and once they were on their way he would receive another payment from Mr. Green.

Rossen and Tomanaga were on needles since they had last seen Ramasavet. Neither of them had gone anywhere, afraid that the call might come while they were out. Their only source of amusement was the hotel bar and then they had to keep their distance and stay on guard. Twice they had been approached by men who outwardly seemed only to want to start a friendly conversation, which always ended up with the question: "And what are you doing in Thailand?" Tommy had gotten a bit tired of this play after a while, and began to answer, "Minding my own fucking business. How about you?"

For him the worst part was the PCOD, the pussy cut-off date. He groaned in his sleep as he dreamed of the lovely, dark-haired, passionate Thai girls. It was an agony to turn down the offers of feminine companionship from the girls who worked the hotel, but he knew full well that this was no time to take a chance on catching anything. It was with—as Rossen had told him—a noticeable lack of self-control that he accepted his monastic fate.

Picking up the receiver, Rossen put an end to the tinny rattling of the phone.

"Hello."

"Good morning, Shooter. It is a clear and welcome day. You and your friend stay where you are. We will have company this evening. I will send my car for you at 2000 hours to take you to where we can meet your new friend and associate with a modicum of privacy. Good-bye."

"Was that Ram?"

Rossen put the receiver back on its cradle. "Yeah. Looks like we might get this thing off the ground yet. I think we're going to meet our escort tonight. Ram's sending a car for us later."

Promptly at 8:00 P.M. a five-year-old Datsun picked them up in front of the hotel. The driver, who was Ram's personal aide, said nothing to them as he wove in and out of traffic, deftly avoiding the tangle of three-wheeled motorbikes, diesel trucks, and oxcarts.

Heading out of the city, the drive took Ploenchit Road past the Erawan to where it turned southeast past the Ambassador Hotel. Taking the road to Pattaya, passing a cluster of wats, they turned off on a dirt road which eventually took them up the driveway of an old rubber plantation once belonging to a French family. Now it was Ramasavet's. The house, like many of those built during colonial times in Asia, was a large, white, rambling structure with broad verandas and latticed windows.

Placed discreetly were several guards wearing olive-drab uniforms and tan berets. All carried automatic rifles. Rossen could feel the sights on him as he got out of the back of the car. Very uncomfortable.

Ram's aide, dressed in khaki cotton trousers and loose shirt, opened the door to the house for them, standing aside to permit them entry. Ram came to them dressed all in white linen. Tomanaga thought he looked like an ice-cream cone but kept the thought to himself.

"Welcome to my house, gentlemen. Please come into the library and meet my other guest."

Standing near a glass-faced cabinet, staring into the case at its contents, was the man they had been waiting for.

"May I present Seng Pouk."

Tomanaga liked what he saw. A dark, small-framed but very tough-looking man. Thick black hair over a strong, sharply angled face. Shaking hands, he felt the strength of the sinews in the thin body. Pouk looked out of place in his American-style jeans and ugly Hawaiian shirt.

"It is good that you have come." His English wasn't bad at all, which would help things considerably as neither of them spoke Thai or any of the mountain dialects.

Ram poured tea all around, serving them himself rather than calling on his household servants, who had been instructed to remain in their quarters until sent for.

"Please be seated, gentlemen, and we will get to the matter at hand."

They found places in hand-woven rattan chairs with broad flowing backs and waited. This was Ram's game for the time being. Let him lay it out the way he wanted.

"To begin, I would like you to know that it has not been easy to make all the arrangements required for an operation such as this. I have had many difficulties but thanks to the Lord Buddha and the calling in of many personal favors, I have been successful."

Rossen wanted to tell him to stop the bullshit, but at least he had said what they wanted to hear: The job was on.

On a table, already laid out in anticipation of their arrival, was a map of the region to which they were to go.

"Gentlemen, if you will join me at the ta-

ble, please, we will go over the logistics of
this plan."

"You"—he indicated Tomanaga and Rossen
—"will go in by private aircraft. Seng Pouk
has already performed a reconnaissance and
selected a drop zone. Your pilot was once
employed by Air America and knows the area
quite well. He has made one flight to the DZ
already; there will be no problem getting you
on-site. All of your equipment is ready. I have
included full survival gear in the event that
you are not able to be exfiltrated by air, as
your Mr. Green requested. If you have no ob-
jections, your departure date will be day after
tomorrow at 0400 hours, which will put you
and Mr. Pouk over the drop zone just at dawn.
Seng Pouk's men will be on-site and signal if
the drop is a go or to be called off."

Satisfied with the way he had taken control of the situation, Ramasavet sat back in
his chair and opened his palms expressively.
"Do you have any questions or comments
about the operation?"

They did. Rossen turned to Pouk, who had
not said another word since their introduc-
tion. "What are the enemy dispositions there?
Where are their outposts? Are they first-line
troops? How much patrolling do they do? What
about enemy aircraft and choppers?"

Pouk nodded his head. On the map he

pointed to several places on both sides of the Laotian border with a calloused finger. "Here. Here. Here. These are infantry camps. Most do not have a strength of over a company. Just to the north of the POW camp, there is another camp which has armored cars and heavy weapons; also, there have been helicopters there at one time or another, but they are not on permanent duty. This camp is the most dangerous. The men there are well trained and disciplined. At the other outposts they are not so good."

Tomanaga touched the POW camp site with his claw. "What else do you have for us about the compound itself? When was the last time you had it under surveillance?"

Pouk shrugged his shoulders. "I do not have much more to add. The last time I was in the vicinity of the camp was five weeks past. Nothing had changed. I did not at that time see any of the Americans there. Since then I have avoided the area; I did not wish to take a chance on putting the Viets on alert. But I have no reason to believe that the Americans have been moved or have died."

Rossen would have liked it better if there had been a more recent sighting but that was the way it was. "Now, how about you, Mr. Pouk. What is your interest in this matter?"

Pouk locked his eyes on the map, which

showed land that had once belonged to his people.

"My reasons are selfish. I want my land back. If you are able to bring out some Americans, then it is possible that your country will come to my people's aid and give us the weapons and money we need to fight the communists. That is the only reason."

Tomanaga interjected, "Where did you learn to speak English?"

Ramasavet answered for him. "Seng Pouk is an educated man who lived in your country for, I believe, six years as part of a student exchange program. He then worked for several American companies as a translator before returning to his homeland and his people. Does that answer your question?"

Tomanaga nodded. "Good enough. Now, we want to go over our gear before taking off, and also we want to resight the rifles and pistols."

Ram smiled pleasantly. "That has already been arranged. You will stay here this night. I have had a range prepared on the far side of my property where you can test your weapons. The rest of your gear will be waiting at the hangar, which conveniently enough is also located on this plantation. You may inspect it before departure. Believe me, it is complete. I am not an amateur, you know!"

"Okay, Ram, don't get your ass in an uproar. We're just doing our jobs, too. Now, what about Green? Has he been notified?"

Ramasavet shook his head. "Not yet. Only when I see that you are physically on your way will I communicate with him."

Ringing a small brass bell brought the khaki-clad aide into the library. Ramasavet nodded graciously. "He will see you to your rooms. Please make yourself at home but do not wander about the grounds. As you can understand, a man in my delicate position does acquire enemies. I would not wish to see an accident befall you."

Seng Pouk stayed behind. Rossen wished he knew what they were talking about. Since the last time they had seen Ram, he had developed a devious feel to him. Perhaps it was just a necessary survival factor for him in a land where no one knows how to give or ask anything in a direct manner. Perhaps not.

They were taken to a room with wide windows leading out to the veranda. Two beds with neatly tucked mosquito netting awaited them. At the foot of each bed were their bags. Ram was efficient. Before closing the door, the aide asked politely, knowing the value of these men to his master, "Do you wish anything, sirs? A drink or food perhaps?"

Rossen looked at Tomanaga, who shook his head from side to side.

"No thanks, we're fine."

Standing at the window, Rossen could hear the cries of night birds and cicadas. A shadow passed a few feet away, crossing the lawn. One of Ramasavet's sentries. Rossen knew the man had looked through the dark at him. There had been a slight change in his motion, a movement of the body which broke the man's forward rhythm. Rossen nodded at him. The man went on.

"Well, looks like we're on the way."

Testing the mattress, Tomanaga began unstrapping his prosthetic appendage. "Looks that way. What do you think about Pouk?"

"Don't know yet. But if I got this figured right, he'll be okay. I think that Ram has his hand deep in Green's pocket and if we come back out, there's probably a hell of a bonus waiting for him. Yeah, Pouk is probably just what Ram said he was. But we'll find out."

He lay down on his bed as Tommy echoed him, "We'll find out. And damned soon, too."

Nine

At the crack of dawn, fresh steaming coffee was brought to them in their room by the same unsmiling khaki-clad aide. "Master Ramasavet is awaiting your presence for breakfast on the veranda, sirs."

As soon as they had finished their coffee and showered they left their room to join Ram for a light meal of melon, mangoes, and pineapple. Rossen had hoped futilely for some bacon and eggs.

Daylight had not brought a lessening of security: Unobstrusive, but there were the guards around the house and gardens.

"Are you ready to check out your equipment, gentlemen?"

Pushing away his plate of half-eaten fruit, Rossen lit up a smoke before answering dryly, "I thought that was what we were here for, Ram."

Nonplussed, Ramasavet took it in stride.

"And so you are." He patted his lips gracefully with a sterile-looking napkin, then tossed it on his plate.

"Then let's do it."

Following him to the front porch, they climbed into the Datsun. He drove them over a dirt road between rows of ill-tended rubber trees, their trunks marred by old scars where they had been cut to permit the white latex to flow into cups.

Ram kep up a running monologue on how difficult it was to get good help, which he needed to restore the plantation to its former glory. Tomanaga fell asleep, head jerking in time with the chock holes.

Ahead of them the trees thinned. Before reaching the clearing Ramasavet hit the horn twice. He didn't have to explain it, but Rossen wondered just how many men Ram kept around to provide him with security.

Leaving the trees, they came onto a flat,

cleared section of land about a hundred meters wide and three hundred long. Running down the middle was a runway. On the south side was a small hangar with a few fifty-gallon fuel drums set apart from it. That was where Ram took them. Stooping in front of the hangar, he hit the horn once more. The doors were swung wide by two soldiers toting M-16s. Inside, it took a moment for their eyes to adjust to the change in light. A twin-engine Beech waited there. Rossen didn't know much about planes, but he could tell one thing: The aircraft was clean. The paint wasn't chipped, everything on it was clean. He took that as a good sign.

Leading them over to a locked wire enclosure, Ram removed a brass key and opened the door, holding it wide for them.

"Inside is your gear. Help yourself."

The weapons were their first concern. The scoped rifles were each stored in hard vinyl cases. Opening the cases, they found the silenced pistols lying in slots in the foam lining. Another box yielded their ammunition and magazines. Squatting down, they filled two clips for each of the weapons, including the pistols. That would be more than enough to sight in the weapons and test the rifles on full auto.

Ram waited for them outside, smoking a cigarette. He butted it out when they came back into the light.

"I see you found your toys. Now, if you will just walk to the back of the building, you will find a firing range has been prepared."

They did as he said. Two tables had been prepared with sandbags ready, for them to rest their rifles on. Running the same north direction as the runway were burns set at one, three, and five hundred meters. In front of each of the burns was a mixed bag of targets. Bulls to zero and man-sized silhouettes.

Settling down on the firing benches behind their tables, each first tore down his piece then put it back together. As always, Stroesser had done superlative work. The weapons went together as though the parts were made of silk instead of steel.

Slapping clips in, they each jacked a round into the chamber. Rossen set his sight on the bull at the hundred-meter mark. The Shephard sight circle for the hundred-meter range exactly on the black dot of the bull. He pulled off one round.

The shot hit one inch to the left and two up.

The thing he liked best about the scope was one-shot zeroing. Adjusting the cross hairs, he moved it over to where it compensated for the difference between the bullet hit and the center of the bull. The sight was ready. One more round at the hundred-meter. A dead hit in the center of the black, then three more at each of the different ranges. All were in the black. The rifle was ready.

Tomanaga had no problems with his; the rifle was dead on zero. Before switching to the pistols, they burned up the rest of the rifle ammo at full auto. No malfunctions.

Each fired one magazine using reflex shooting at close range to test out the silencers, then moved back inside the hangar where the shadows made the beam of the infrared sights easier to see. Again there were no problems. The pistols whispered and the sights were right on. Stroesser had done things right.

Once they were satisfied with their weapons, they went through the rest of the gear laid out on the hangar floor. Shortwave R/T with extra batteries and crystals. Medic kit with antibiotics and dressings in the event the POWs were injured or ill. Jungle survival kit in case they had to walk out. Dehydrated rations, machetes, camouflage uniforms, and, in one box, a stack of RPG-7s and rockets, along with several other boxes containing grenades and ammo for AK-47s.

Ram's voice came out of the gloom. "We're going to send with you a few things for Pouk's men."

One by one they went through each item, checking it carefully.

Standing up and dusting off his knees, Rossen said, "Okay, Ram. It looks good. We're ready when you are, I guess." He looked questioningly at Tomanaga, who nodded agreement.

Each of them took a set of camouflage utilities with them; they wouldn't be wearing civvies for a while. Escorting them back outside, Ram closed the hangar doors and locked them.

"If there is nothing else, then, you leave before dawn. At that time I shall introduce you to your pilot. Until then the rest of the day is yours. I suggest that you get as much rest as possible."

The ride back to the house was made in silence. It was deep-think time, trying to recall if they had missed anything that would be needed later. It was always tough to figure out just what to take. You didn't want to be caught short and you didn't want to overload, because you'd have to carry everything on your back. They couldn't find anything wrong with the issue; Ram did know his business. Everything they had to carry was essential; there was no wasted weight.

As Ramasavet had suggested, they spent most of the day flat on their backs or sitting on their beds looking at the maps and photos. Rossen was getting edgy; he hadn't smoked a cigarette since the one he'd had instead of breakfast. Time to quit again.

At their option, they had supper in their rooms, not wishing to be bored by Ramasavet again. The man had become an incredible bore. With any luck at all he might even be the premier of Thailand one day.

Seng Pouk had been taking care of his business. He had attended a meeting with several other tribal leaders who were conducting guerrilla raids into Cambodia and Laos. As always, nothing was resolved. Everyone wanted everyone else to do things their way. He wondered if they would ever get together on anything. A unified command and policy was absolutely necessary if they were to make any progress against the common enemy. It was a weary and dejected man who returned to the plantation. Sometimes he thought it was all an exercise in futility, but he had no choice. He had to go on. There had been too much of his people's blood spilled for him to ever stop. Only death could stop his battle.

Something had to be done, something dramatic, to draw the attention of the world to the situation in Southeast Asia. If that could be done, then perhaps the Americans would come back. If the tribal leaders couldn't pick one of their own to lead them, then Americans could do it for them. That would solve the first difficulty; then they could deal with the rest.

Stopping only to pay his respects to Ramasavet, he too went to his room to rest. The room was confining, too close, stuffy; after years in the jungle, it was hard for him to accept walls of stone and brick. Giving up, he took a blanket and put it on the floor of the porch. There at last he could sleep.

A blue haze settled over the room as they lay there listening to each other's breathing. It was hard to let sleep come. There were too many thoughts in the mind. Too many things to go wrong. Too much for which there was no answer—those would only come after they were committed.

Neither was aware of when the other's breathing slowed. It was only with a soft rap on their door that they knew they had fallen into sleep.

"Yeah, we're getting up."

The door opened as Ram's aide brought them coffee in a silver service. Hot, black, steaming, it helped to clear the fuzz which lay around the edges of the mind.

By the time they had dressed, Ram was waiting impatiently with Pouk in the car. "Please hurry. You must be over the LZ at first light."

They climbed in. Pouk's dark face was a silent mask, though he did give them a small smile of greeting. The predawn was a time for little speech.

The night seemed even darker around the twin beams of the headlights as Ramasavet wove his way unerringly through the dark bodies of the rubber trees, again honking his horn to let those on watch know of his approach.

This time the hangar door was open as they came to a stop.

From the hangar a grumbling, blurred voice harangued them. "Well, let's get on with it. Goddamn it to hell, I want to be in and out before noon."

Mentally, Rossen groaned. Their pilot, one Amos Harding, was obviously a lush, with a face that matched his voice.

When he removed the pint of Jim Beam from his lips, he caught Rossen's look. "Don't let that bother you. I've flown everything with wings one time or another, and most of the time drunk as a judge. So let's just get on with the job. Get your asses on board. I've already stored your gear. C'mon. Let's go, let's go!"

Ram stood where his face couldn't be seen, but Rossen and Tomanaga knew he was grinning. There was nothing to do about it. They had gone too far to change plans.

Pointing his trigger finger at Ram, Rossen whispered, "I owe you one for this."

He didn't hear Ramasavet's response because of the engines starting.

Harding taxied out the hangar door in a cloud of dust, and turned sharply to the right, lining up on the north side of the strip. His passengers strapped themselves into seats; helpless now, they had to leave things to Harding. They felt him lock the brakes and rev the engines a time or two until they smoothed out; then he gave it the throttle, building up to max revs, and cut the brakes loose. They were off the deck in ten seconds, rising up into the night clouds.

As soon as the plane steadied, Rossen released himself from the seat belts and went forward, flinching when he saw Harding remove a now empty bottle from his lips.

"Sit down, Shooter. I don't know your name but that's what Ramasavet calls you."

Adjusting the trim a bit, Harding took another bottle from the side pocket of his trouser leg. They had gone above the clouds to where the night was clear. A half moon nearing the edge of the earth gave off a cool light. By it, through the windshield, Rossen got his first good look at their pilot. He'd been a handsome man once. Now the nose had broken veins crisscrossing it, and the face had a fullness to it that wasn't healthy.

"Don't try to analyze me, boy. If anything kills you, it won't be me. I know to the drop exactly how much to take to reach my maximum proficiency and I won't go a milliliter over till I'm back on 'terra not so firma.'" He offered Rossen a pull from his bottle, which was refused. Harding shrugged. "You might as well take it easy while you can. We got about an hour and a half to go. It's not all that far direct, but I'm having to do a little maneuvering to avoid some known installations on the way. We wouldn't want a MIG to keep us company, now, would we?"

Rossen agreed that it would be best if they did things his way. Harding took one half-sip and, to Rossen's relief, put the bottle away.

"That's it. Everything's just right. Now, why don't you go back with your friends and wait. I like to drive by myself. When we're ready to set down, I'll let you know."

They waited. There was no talk; they simply sat. That was all that could be done. Their first indication that they were getting near the DZ was when Harding roared, "Next stop in three minutes. Get your shit together and get ready to get off my fucking plane so I can go home and get decently drunk."

From the rear of the plane it was still night, but in the cockpit dawn had begun to break over Vietnam. The plane began its descent, passing through the first layer of clouds. Harding yelled back again, "We got the signal to come on in. Three lights dead ahead. This'll be a straight run. As soon as I reach the far end and turn around I want you off!"

Rossen yelled back, "Listen, smart ass, when we're on the deck you're on my turf, so watch it!"

Harding laughed good-naturedly. "Well, well! That is true all right. It is certainly true but just remember this before you let your bulldog mouth overload your canary ass. I'm the one who's supposed to come back for you."

Rossen could find no proper response and shut up.

The landing gear went down. Seconds later they touched, bounced, and touched again. Harding cut back on the throttle and hit the brakes. Things happened so fast it was hard to register; the next thing they knew the pilot was swearing at them again to get their shit and get off.

Pouk opened the door. On the deck it was still dark. Hands from the outside reached up to take the bundles he tossed out, then he went out, followed by Tomanaga and Rossen. Harding was turning around before Rossen's feet hit the earth, his props blowing clouds of dust, grass, and leaves into their faces. The men on the ground covered their faces with their hands until the Beech was away and climbing back up into what Harding considered the relative safety of the skies.

Dark figures surrounded them as Pouk was thumped on the back and greeted by his men. Now it was his turn to take command and he did.

"We go now. There are many miles to travel and we must be far away from this place before the sun is full up."

Grabbing their packs and weapons, Rossen and Tomanaga put full mags into their pieces and jacked a round into the chamber. That was the last sound other than that of labored breathing and tread of feet on the soft spongy floor of the jungle.

They were on their way.

————————————**Ten**

Ground mist was rising from the spongy jungle floor by the time it was light enough to see clearly. Pouk had been met by eleven of his men. To the untrained eye they would have appeared a ragtag batch of bandits. Rossen and Tommy saw something else. True, they had no uniforms and wore a bastardized mixture of mountain tribal dress and parts of uniforms from several armies; one even had a World War II British bush jacket with the insignia of some royal regiment or another sewn to the shoulder. It was the way they handled their weapons and moved which set them apart. Somewhere they'd had training. Good training.

Pouk placed the two Americans in the center of their small column, where they would have the best protection. The first half day's march was the worst. Once the initial adrenaline rush was over, and their legs had finished the worst of their protesting, they settled in, but it was a job to keep up with the Mnong tribesmen. Their legs were just long whipped bands of steel muscle. All their lives they had gone up and down these hills and valleys. They had a way of moving that no Westerner could ever learn.

They left sign as they passed but not much; nothing to draw any special interest if a dink patrol came across their trail. Behind him, Rossen saw that the Mnong tribesman bringing up drag made a constant effort to cover the sign that his large booted feet were leaving on the trail. A size eleven boot would definitely be out of the ordinary where most men wore no more than a six or seven.

Twice they stopped to lay dogo while a chopper flew on by. It sounded like a Huey, but Rossen couldn't be sure. It went over too fast and the heavy tree cover kept him from seeing more than a fleeting shadow. It did say one thing: The Charlies were still patrolling by air. Pouk came to them after the first chopper went by.

"No sweat. They make two runs over this region every day. Their route varies a little but they always return to their bases before dark."

Pouk smiled a bit. "That is, they do now. We shot down two of their helicopters last month when they came out after dark. None of their crews ever returned. It has made them a bit cautious; now they leave the night to us. It is much the same as they once did to the American forces in Vietnam. Now it is reversed and we are the guerrillas, with the advantages that it gives us in mobility and timing. Those are the only advantages we have."

Pouk didn't push them too hard after the first day's march, giving them a chance to get their legs back. Steadily, though, wasting no time, Seng Pouk led them unerringly through a maze of trails and fields, across rivers and up the rocky, vine-covered mountainsides to their destination. Rossen knew they were taking the long way in case their trail was cut, making it more difficult for whoever found it to be able to determine their destination. Hopefully, the trip back would be shorter. It would mean they had been successful.

When Pouk finally pointed to a mountain across a narrow valley and said, "That is where we can see the camp from," Rossen's relief was almost palpable.

Hocking their packs higher on their shoulders to ease the cramps building up between their shoulder blades, they began the last climb.

It took almost total concentration for Rossen to not scratch at the sores on his face where he had been lashed by thorn vines and bitten by every kind of goddamned insect the jungle housed. Everything on him ached. He had sores under the armpits, where dirt and salt-encrusted seams had rubbed him raw. He knew Tomanaga wasn't in any better shape. The last two days' march had been a bitch. Even with the porters their load had nearly broken their backs, climbing up and down jungle trails, crossing streams and rivers that weren't on anybody's map. But at last they were where they could see the camp.

Tomanaga slid up alongside Rossen, handing him the binoculars. Adjusting the focus on the 8-by-30 Bushnells, he brought the camp into focus. It was laid out in the shape of a triangle, with an eight-foot-tall barrier fence of barbed wire with aprons of concertina on all sides. Three tall guard towers, one gate. Three structures outside, probably where the guards stayed. Across the road a better built structure with stuccoed white walls and tiled roof, probably the HQ for the brass. Inside the compound were half a dozen more buildings constructed of bamboo and palm thatch with woven mats for sides, built up three or four feet off the ground.

Scoping out the area to the north, Rossen could see where the side of a mountain was being scooped out. Red earth stood in marked contrast to the jungle green. The captives inside the camp were most likely being used as slave labor to either work a rock quarry or dig gravel for the road he saw cutting across the outside of the compound leading north and east.

They would have to get closer to the compound, closer . . . but not now. It was time to rest; even the Mnong porters were played out. He felt the anticipation but knew that they would have to rest for at least two days to get their strength back before they made the hit on the compound. And that would only come down if they were certain that one or more MIAs were still being held there.

Nudging Tomanaga's shoulder, he pointed down the side of the hill to a narrow animal trail, then pointed to himself. Tomanaga nodded, understanding. Sliding over the crest of the ridge, Rossen worked his way in a low crawl to the trail, keeping to the sides of it, and disappeared from view. Tomanaga kept watch on the space separating the base of the mountain and the camp. There was a cleared area of low grass between the brush line at the foot of the mountain and the camp. A distance of about two thousand meters where there was little stand-up cover. Through the glasses he could see a thin line running about a thousand meters in the direction of the camp, then veering off to the west. The animal trail.

Flies found him. Buzzing around his face, they whined and hummed; he stoically accepted them as just another test of his patience and endurance. One settled in his ear, buzzing fiercely, sending incredible vibrations against his tympanic membrane. He slapped, crushing the pest into pulp. *Fuck a bunch of Oriental stoicism.*

Rossen was gone forty minutes, then came back up the mountainside, still taking advantage of all possible cover until he was back in his original position with Tomanaga.

"The trail's clear; no sign of booby traps. There's fresh animal sign all the way down. Let's get back to the others."

Scooting backward until they were clear of the horizon, they rejoined the Mnong.

"Okay, let's set up camp here. I didn't see any sign that the Viets have been up here. Just keep it a cold camp. No fires, no smoke or talking unless it's necessary. Let's keep it quiet."

The Mnong nodded their heads, and several smiled, showing betel-nut-stained teeth. Good tough men. Rossen wished them well, thinking about the shock of dropping from one level of civilization into another: from the world of jets and rockets and men on the moon to a place where people had never ridden in a wheeled vehicle, where offerings were made to the spirits of fields and streams and parents thought it was natural for their children to be covered with sores.

Tomanaga set pickets out as the rest found places to hole up, stringing their hammocks between trees and wriggling into them. They all needed sleep; no one ate. The day's march had taken the desire for food out of them. That would come later.

Checking his watch, Rossen saw that they still had about three hours to nightfall; some time after that he and Tomanaga would go down to the compound and check it out. Until then he needed his sleep, too. Tying up his jungle hammock, he climbed in, pulling the mosquito mesh over him, his weapon on his chest. Tomanaga would take first watch. Even with the Mnong it was best to have one of them awake at all times. He'd sleep for a few hours, then let Tomanaga do the same. After that they would go down the mountain.

He didn't know when sleep claimed him. The last thing he remembered was blinking his eyes. The next thing he knew, Tomanaga was tapping him gently on the sole of his boot. .

"Yeah, Tommy, I'm awake." Groaning with stiff bones and aching muscles, he relinquished the hammock to Tomanaga.

Stretching his back and arms to limber up, Rossen walked the perimeter. The pickets were wide awake. Whispering to them that he was going back up on the ridge for another look at the camp, he clambered back up the slope until he reached the place he and Tomanaga had been earlier. There on the ridge a breeze found its way to cool his face and ease the itching of the bites and scratches. From his canteen he poured a small amount of water onto his neckerchief with which to wash away the salt and crud that had collected around the rims of his eyes.

Refocusing the binoculars, he scoped out the camp and buildings once more. There wasn't much to see. From the windows outside the camp he could see reddish glows. Probably from lamps. Nearly all cooking was done outside; the bamboo and thatch huts were too flammable to have fire inside them. The smell of woodsmoke drifted up to him. Yeah, there it was: smoldering coals near the largest of the outside huts. A cooking fire which was dying down. Wishing he could do the whole job from this distance, he slid back away from the ridge.

He wanted to think, to get a feel for the place and go over what info he had, which was precious little. Supposedly there were at least two Americans in the compound, possibly more. In a way he hoped there wouldn't be any more. It was going to be tough enough to get one or two well men out, but with three or four you could bet your ass that some of them would be sick and have to be carried out. He hoped he wouldn't have to make the decision to leave anyone behind.

He still had a while to wait before waking Tomanaga. Taking advantage of it, he went to his pack, rummaged around in it, and found his cleanest pair of dirty socks. Sitting down on a soft grassy mound, he took his boots off—just the easing of pressure when he undid the laces was excruciatingly delicious. When the odor hit him, he almost put them back on. Peeling his socks off, he examined his feet.

They were wrinkled like very old and dead fish. Pale, sickly white, and wrinkled. Nearly groaning with pleasure, he began to rub them, getting some circulation back into the abused limbs. Setting them down on the earth, the feel of cool dew on grass was better than pussy as he wiggled his toes in it.

Sighing deeply, he lay back on the mound, facing the night skies. Looking through the dark canopy of leaves, he could make out the stars, cold and distant. They looked strange. In this part of the world there was no Big Dipper or Orion. Other constellations had taken their place, he didn't know much about them, other than the Southern Cross. It was just good to lie down and rest. A distant roaring cacophony brought his head around to face the south. Then he recognized the sound. Monkeys fussing and fighting, nothing to worry about unless the noise came closer. It was a good night. They had come a long way and their goal was almost in hand. The idea of the killing that was to come didn't bother him. It was normal, expected; something he could deal with more easily than trying to do his taxes stateside.

Lying there, he thought about the hundreds of nights when he and Tomanaga had been out, either on the hardballs or working with one or another unit as countersnipers. Those years seemed much closer tonight than they had only a few weeks ago. The only difference was he was older and time had taken its toll. He hurt more and didn't move as fast as he once had, and he wanted to smoke, something that had never bothered him in Nam. Time was always going to be the winner. You could fight it, hold it back, but it would win.

To the east a distant crackling in the night told him heat storms were rumbling over the mountains of the central highlands of Vietnam. Almost due west, less than eighty miles away, was Kontum, and a little farther south was Gia Lai or, as it was better known to Americans, Pleiku. Names that brought him little pleasure but no regrets.

He pulled back the Velcro flap on his watch face: 0100 hours. The guard shift had probably taken place.

Waking Tomanaga, he gave him time to get oriented, eat a handful of cold rice, and take a leak before getting ready to move out. Camouflage sticks were applied to the face and hands to cut down on reflection and make it easier for them to blend with the night. Brush and leaves were stuck on their fatigues to break up the outline of their bodies, and the barrels of their rifles were wrapped in burlap to reduce shine and break up their outlines also. All gear taped down tight, nothing rattled or shook. As usual, they tested this by jumping up and down vigorously several times. They were ready. To the Mnong leader Rossen said, "Keep alert, but don't get trigger-happy. I don't know how long we're going to be, so just be careful and don't go killing any moving bushes before you know who it is. We might not be able to get back until tomorrow night. If any shooting starts around the camp, just stay low till we get back. If we don't get back within an hour of the shooting, then you and your men move on out. We won't be coming."

Seng Pouk nodded, knowing what he meant. Back on the ridge, Rossen scoped out the area once with the Starlight, then moved ahead down the animal trail. Night birds and bats whisked wraithlike through the treetops; the only other movement came from the small breeze and their feet as they passed over the trail heading down to the flats where they would have to cross the two thousand meters to the camp. Neither of them expected much to happen until dawn. That was when the prisoners, if there were any, would most likely be lined up for roll call or work detail. Until then they would go over the surrounding terrain making a chart of every hollow and dip, every clump of brush or patch of bamboo that could serve as cover. Then they would move closer to the camp and wait.

Stopping every few minutes, they would scope out the area again, taking their time. It wasn't likely that the Viets would have any sentries posted here; they had little to fear this far inside their own area of control. If this was a POW camp, then the men on duty were probably the same as prison guards, and not expecting any outside trouble.

In a rough spiral, they began their recon. Tomanaga made marks on a piece of brown paper indicating where they could find cover or where there was an obstacle. The house with the tiled roof was the only difficulty they had. It was guarded by two men at the door and two others who made constant circuits around the house; all were armed with AK-47s. They were alert: Several times the two men on roving guard moved away from the house to investigate small noises. They gave them space and moved on. The spiral brought them within a hundred meters of the barbed-wire fence, where they found a low mound with a bush in front of it. From there they would be a few feet above the floor of the camp.

With bayonets they dug a hole behind the bush, taking care to move the fresh dirt away and scatter it so any careful eye would not see any difference in the colors around the site. It took an hour and a half to complete the task, then it was crawl in, lay low, and wait for the sun to rise. Again, Tomanaga took first watch, letting Rossen sleep.

Through the scope, he checked out the guard towers, bringing the sentries into focus. They were very casual—they smoked and they talked easily, unconcerned, seldom looking toward the outside of the wire and not paying much attention to the inside. Twice he saw a pair of guards go from one hut to another carrying a lantern. They would go inside for a few minutes, then return. There was one hut to which no one went.

Swinging the Starlight over to his left, he centered on the largest of the outside huts. In the glow of the scope there came a brighter image, a haze from inside the hut. A lantern was on low. No movement.

He gave his eyes a break and opened his ears. In the dark, sound carries. He could hear the voices of the Viets clearly as they talked. One laughed. Tomanaga wondered if he knew the joke.

Rossen was laid out beside him, head at the entrance of their hole in the earth to take advantage of the breeze. Small muscles moved of their own volition as he slept, twitching at the side of his jaw and the temple. What did he dream of, this man to whom he had attached himself? Did he dream of women or drink? Or did he dream of falling, falling into the deep places of the mind where terror sleeps with a sign on the door: DO NOT DISTURB.

Before dawn, Tomanaga switched over to the ART, taking it slowly along the wire. The Viets had become careless, or perhaps they were so confident that their prisoners had no will left in them that they didn't need to keep things up. There were few trip wires and a couple of mines in the wire; others could be seen on the camp side of the barrier, their prongs sticking up above the earth where the rains of past years had washed away the covering soil. No problem. On his chart, Tomanaga marked the places where the mines were located. The Viets would regret not performing primary maintenance, being sloppy.

Blaring noise brought Rossen's head up quickly, eyes instantly focused, hand to the trigger of his weapon as he rolled over on his stomach, bringing the M-14 to his shoulder. Tomanaga's hand touched him and pointed. A loudspeaker on a pole was giving off a scratchy, discordant rendition of the Vietnamese national anthem, the "Victory of Dien Bien Phu." More men were in evidence now, guards entering the compound in twos and fours.

By the huts, outside cooking fires were being stirred into life. This was it. In a few minutes they'd know. Putting the rifle down, Rossen replaced it with the binoculars.

———————————————— **Eleven**

The door to the first hut in the compound opened, then the others. From them, men started to stumble out into the brightness of day. Limbs dangling, loose-jointed, heads down submissively. All Orientals. Guards hustled them along into a semblance of a line, striking with bamboo batons at anyone who moved too slowly. Adjusting the image in his range finder, Rossen scoped the door of the second hut. It was open. Two guards, one on each side of the door. The interior of the hut was too dark for him to make out any detail in his scope. Suddenly, a figure stumbled forward wearing ragged black pajamas. He was a small man, maybe an inch or two taller than his captors, and he moved with the gait of an old, arthritic man, but he was clearly a Caucasian.

Rossen nudged Tomanaga. "We got one!" Then came another, taller man, around six feet, who could barely move. The weight of his emaciated body was too much for him to carry. He made it down the steps, then fell loose-limbed to the earth. Unceremoniously, the guards summoned two of the Oriental inmates to drag him back inside. The standing Caucasian was marched over to join the Asians. As soon as he was in line, the column did a right face and marched out of the compound, stopping at the gate to take up shovels and picks on their way. Work detail!

Rossen pulled back inside their hole, tugging Tomanaga with him.

"Well, we got two of them, buddy. We'll keep an eye on the camp, and check out its routines and the time of the guard changes, and try and get the numbers on them. Then we'll pull out as soon as it's dark."

Once the inmates were gone, the camp went back to what appeared to be its normal, somewhat lethargic, profile. Several times men came and went. From the large house outside the wire he saw women. He wished the distance were closer so he could get a better look at their faces. Even at this distance, though, he knew they were good-looking women by the way they carried themselves. Each was wearing the traditional Ao Dai of Vietnam in pastel colors, with their dark, raven hair flowing loose to the shoulders. From the steps they waved good-bye to the two obvious officer types who were picked up by a military car. Rossen couldn't determine exactly what kind, though it might have been a Russian Zis. They left at 1000 hours and were returned at 1335 hours. Judging by the time and what he knew of the area, he figured that they probably went to either the military outpost five clicks away or to Muong May on the same road, about thirty clicks to the northeast. That was the nearest large town. Anything farther than that and they couldn't have gotten back till nightfall.

The prisoners were brought back an hour before sundown, and after stacking their tools at the gate, they were lined up to be fed from a communal pot, given ten minutes to eat whatever it was, then taken back to their huts and locked up.

Rossen kept his eye on the short American when he was brought back. Through the expanded vision of the binoculars, he caught one blurred look at the man's face. It reminded him of pictures he had seen when the Allies liberated the concentration camps at Auschwitz and Buchenwald. Disgusted, he put the glasses down. "Okay, Tomanaga, that's our main target. There's no way to tell about the tall guy's condition, but the short one is going out with us."

As soon as it was full dark, they left their hole, making their way back up the mountain. By the time they were challenged by Seng Pouk, at the perimeter of the camp, they were thoroughly tired, thirsty, and hungry, and both had to take a killer crap. They had been afraid to relieve themselves in their hole. It was just a hair too close, and the wind was not in their favor.

Tomanaga filled Pouk in on what they had seen. The Mnong's dark face lit up. "We go, then?"

Tomanaga nodded. "Yeah, we go. Maybe tomorrow night. I'll have to ask Rossen about that." He would have, but Rossen had already found his hammock and was down for the count. Pouk led Tomanaga over to his hammock and told him to get some rest. "We shall take the watch this night. Have no fear. My people have been fighting for too many years against the foreigners to become careless. It is important to us that you get one of your men out. It will prove to the world what kind of animals the communists are. Then perhaps they will help us to throw them out of our highlands."

Tomanaga mumbled something about hoping that Pouk was right, then he too was out.

The rumbling of their empty stomachs aroused them at midmorning. By each of them squatted a Mnong warrior, his weapon ready. They both felt a bit odd at having these small fierce men watch over them in their sleep.

For the Mnong, the responsibility given to them for the safety of these men was paramount. It went without saying that they would have readily given their lives for the foreigners because that is exactly what Pouk had told them to do if they were threatened. For some reason they couldn't fathom, these two strange men were important. They would do as they were told.

Atwood lay down his chopsticks and sipped from a glass of good French Chenin Blanc. His control officer, Comrade Colonel Cao Lam Phang, was, as always, an excellent host.

He felt more comfortable after taking off his regulation uniform. He admired the epaulets with the insignia of major on them. In the American army his highest rank was corporal. But he was infinitely more comfortable in the black loose-fitting pajamas and open slippers than in the stiff khaki dress.

Phang toasted his guest and the ladies with an upraised glass.

"Live long, live well, my friends." To Atwood he made a side toast. "And to you especially, I give felicitations. You have done well. Never have you failed in your missions, and for this, our superiors are most grateful, as witnessed by our promotions and the special considerations they have given us."

Personally, Atwood wasn't too thrilled with the considerations. A few cases of wine, a house of their own, but stuck in the boondocks with an occasional trip to Hong Kong or Singapore for a little R&R. Big fucking deal! But he wouldn't have gone back to the States and the life he had left for anything. Here he was someone important, and he had power. He could kill without any bullshit military red tape or civilian remorse. He wondered if Phang knew of the deal he had made with General Trang. For every successful mission, twenty thousand American dollars were deposited to numbered accounts in Swiss and Belgian banks. One day, when he felt that his usefulness was coming to an end, he would go on a mission and just disappear, taking his money and fading away somewhere to spend it in a more civilized style.

Until then this life served him well enough, and there were many things to enjoy, not the least of which was fucking over Carlson, the smart-ass, self-righteous air force major in hut two. He had helped break him till he was little more than a mass of autonomic nerves. Pavlov would have loved him.

He had told Carlson long ago to stay off his ass when they were both POWs in the same camp in northern Laos. Now Atwood was making him pay and it felt good, really fucking good. One of these days he would put him out of his misery by shooting him in the nape of the neck, but not just yet.

Phang caught the pensive expression on his face. "Something amuses you, my friend?"

Atwood shook his head. "Just thinking about Carlson."

Phang nodded his head sagely. "I know that you have a great distaste for that one. I tell you what I shall do. An extra bonus for you. I here and now make a gift to you of the man. He is yours to do with as you please."

Laughing, they toasted the arrangement. Another bottle of wine was opened. For an Oriental, Phang had a prodigious capacity for the grape, and these sessions often lasted through the night with the ladies giving their favors equally between them in the best spirit of comradely sharing.

For the men in the hills it was a day and night of sleep, rest, and preparation. Each man had his assignment. Two men for each guard tower. Two more for the barracks. Two for backup, each of whom had an RPG-7 and his personal weapon. And Rossen and Tomanaga, who would actually go in for the prisoners.

Eight times they had gone over the plan, keeping it as simple as possible. They would try to keep this from becoming a shoot-'em-up ballbuster. If possible they would get in and get out before the Viets knew they were there. Killing was to be held to a minimum unless the shit broke loose. That's when the RPGs would come into play. As for the radio, it would not be used until after the raid, when, one way or another, they would have to have the plane come in for them. If they got back.

From their packs, Rossen and Tomanaga removed two odd-looking pistols with what appeared to be extra-heavy barrels. They were silenced .22-caliber Ruger automatics with full clips of hollow-point rounds that had been loaded with fulminate of magnesium to make them explosive. At ten feet the only sound they made was the swishing of a light breeze through dry leaves. Mounted on each was a laser sight. Where the red dot of the laser touched was where the bullet would strike. Only Rossen took his M-14. Tomanaga exchanged his rifle for one of the AKs in case they needed some rapid-fire power.

Once more all was checked and rechecked. Everything that could make a sound was either removed or taped down. Faces repainted, weapons given a last check—they were ready. If their timing was right, at around 0400 hours they would move inside the compound, going through the wire. Rossen slapped his kit bag, feeling the large cutters inside along with the extras he would need. The hour had been chosen because that was when the ground fog in the hollows and low places would be at its thickest. The fog would give them time to get in, get their men, and get back out, still leaving them enough time to make it into the jungle before the enemy got wise.

Tomanaga nudged him, then rubbed the side of his own face with his leather-covered claw. "Sam? I still don't like having all those troops down there able to come after us. I really believe we should take them out first. That way, if anything goes down wrong, we won't have them on our ass later."

Rossen had thought about the same problems; they had discussed it before.

"Okay, Tommy. If that's the way you want it, that's how we'll play it."

He trusted Tomanaga's instincts. Too many times what Tomanaga felt rather than knew had meant the difference between life and death for them. He called Pouk over to him and gave the order for the change in plans. "This shouldn't make over ten minutes' difference either way."

Pouk smiled, the night light gleaming off his shining teeth. He liked it. Whatever brought death to the invaders was fine with him.

"Okay, Pouk, if that goes down all right, take the two men you've put on the barracks and move them to cover the house with the tiles." He checked his watch. It was ten minutes to midnight and they had a way to go. "All right. Let's do it."

Single file, moving silently, they crossed over the top of the ridge and began down the animal trail, fleeting, flickering shadows between the brush, the trunks of trees with the mottled night light seeping through the canopy of leaves over their heads.

They eased down the trail until they reached the field. With prearranged hand signals, Rossen told them to spread out and move toward their targets. The timing was right. Heavy night mist covered most of their bodies, with only heads and occasionally shoulders appearing as dark blots over the wavering, shifting fog. By the time they were halfway across the field, their bodies were soaked, clothes clinging clammily to their skin. The mist chilled them deep, cutting through the surface temperature of their flushed flesh.

Time check: 0230. That was good. They had plenty of time to move slow and easy. Movement was the biggest danger. When you moved fast, things happened, noise was made. Stumps and holes in the ground weren't seen or felt. They would all be in place at 0300 hours. That would give them some time for a breather, to let the pounding of hearts and aching of lungs caused by exertion and anxiety settle down.

Rossen and Tomanaga began to veer over to where the guards' quarters were, and lost sight of the others. Only the occasional muted *thut* of a foot pulling itself from a soft spot said they were not alone. Forty meters from the shack, they went to their bellies. Through the Starlight scope, Rossen saw two men standing on the porch of the shack, smoking and talking quietly. He could only make out one with a weapon; he couldn't tell if the other was armed or not.

Scuttling crabwise to lie closer to Tomanaga, Rossen whispered, "We got to get them off the porch. If one drops his piece, it might

wake up some of the gooks inside the hut.''
Tomanaga nodded in agreement.

Tomanaga went first, inching his way to
within twenty meters, still keeping his body
below the level of the mist. In his good hand
he held the silenced Ruger. Rossen shifted to
flank him by another ten meters. He made a
small dull snap with his fingers. Tomanaga
removed his glove, baring the steel hook. Once,
twice, he tapped it against the butt of the
Ruger. The men on the porch made no move.
He repeated the sound, louder.

One of the men turned his head, facing out
toward them. Rossen knew he was questioning the sound. Then he went back to talking
to his comrade.

*Goddamn that ignorant motherfucker, was he
stone deaf?*

Tomanaga tapped once more. This time the
armed guard placed his AK under his arm,
one hand on the foregrip, and leaned forward,
his dark eyes straining to pierce the mist and
gloom. The man with him reached behind
and also came up with a weapon. By their
body English they weren't frightened, just cautiously curious. The first man took a step
forward.

That's it! Come to Papa! Rossen mentally
pushed him onward off the porch to where
the ground was soft and the sound of falling

bodies and weapons would not be heard. The guard came off the porch, followed by the other. Holding their weapons at the hip, they each turned, facing into the dark, heads cocked, trying to figure out what and where the sound was. They came forward five more steps to the edge of the grass. That was it.

Rising up from the mist just enough to see, Rossen leveled the Ruger. The red beam of the laser sight settled on the forehead of the first man. Another beamed between the eyes of the second man: Tomanaga was with him.

Each of the guards looked at the other with wonder. What was the red glowing mark that the other wore? They were still questioning it when their minds went out of business. *Phhht, phhht*. Four times, two rounds for each man. The small .22-caliber hollow points entered the red dots on the targets' heads, poking neat pencil-sized openings in each man's skull, then exploding into fragments once they had made entry. The two men slumped to the damp earth, fingers jerking open, unable to pull triggers. Rossen didn't know what it was, but there was something about a brain shot that caused the fingers to jerk open instead of closing, and they had given each of the guards two shots in the head. Rossen let loose his breath, glad it had begun. The opening act was always the toughest. Now that they had started, it would get better.

Tomanaga moved out of the mist, stopping only to fire one more round each into the heads of the two already dead men. It was always best to make sure. Changing clips as he moved to the porch, he stopped and listened for any sound from inside the hut. Nothing, nothing at all. Everything was silent save for the breathing of the men in their sleep. Making a circle with his laser, he motioned for Rossen to join him. Rossen's heavier weight caused the boards on the porch to creak obscenely loud. Stopping, he listened again. Nothing. The men inside were dead asleep. He smiled at the joke he'd made.

Softly, Tomanaga opened the bamboo door and stepped inside. Rossen followed, taking the left side of the barracks with Tomanaga on the right. It was time. Looking down the two rows of sleeping men, their faces hazed by mosquito nets, Rossen pushed back feeling. They were targets, not people, that was all. In unison they moved to their first targets and placed the Rugers a foot away from the men's faces where the mosquito net would slow up the ejected cases. Red dots appeared on the sleeping foreheads. *Phht, phht.* An about-face and they were at the next target. Repeat. Again and again, they worked their way down the rows of sleeping men, stopping once each to change clips. When they finished, all the men inside were truly dead asleep. Twenty-two men in forty-three seconds. There would be no interference from them.

Sweat ran freely down both men's faces, small pools collecting in the hollows between the nose and upper lip. Rossen shook his off like a dog. "Okay, Tommy, let's get to the rest of it."

Slipping back outside the barracks, they moved into the cover presented by the ground mist. They had picked the guard tower on the west end of the camp as their place of entry.

In the comforting shelter of the mist, they inched their way closer to the western guard tower. Easy does it. Do nothing in a hurry. Take in your breath through the nose. Control the pounding of the heart, try to ease the adrenaline flow that makes you want to get up on your feet, and rush, scream, do anything except crawl like slugs.

The mist lay along the stands of concertina wire on the outer apron. Tomanaga moved forward. He had memorized the positions of the mines and trip wires, but he still moved cautiously. There was always a chance that he had missed something. Above them they could hear the guards talking quietly, as men did in the small hours of the predawn when the earth was heavy with sleep.

Pouk waited also, fingers tightening at the cry of every night bird or cicada, wishing he was with the two long-noses. It would have been better than this sitting and waiting.

Others waited in the house of the red tiles as Atwood and Phang emptied another bottle. The women now were naked and sleeping on mats on the floor. Atwood eyed his superior, his control officer. "You said that son of a bitch was mine, didn't you?"

Phang nodded, blinking thick lids. "*Xa phai*, yes, he is yours to do with as you wish. I have said it, therefore it is so."

Atwood rose from his chair, staggering to the door. "Good, then I want him here now. I want to see him, teach him who his master is."

Phang laughed, thinking: And they say that Asians are a cruel people. We have nothing to better this sadist. This opportunist who would betray us as fast as he did his own race if it was to his advantage. One day I will also have to teach him what the word "master" means. Until then he has value and we will humor his whims.

He called to the sentries outside, ordering

them to go to the camp and bring the one
called Carlson to him.

Rossen was through the first apron of wire
as Tomanaga kept watch on the tower, his
Ruger at the ready in case one of the guards
turned to look at the wire or became overly
curious at the muted twang of wires being
cut. This was the touchiest part. They had
been hesitant to shoot the guards this early in
the game. Rossen snipped through a wire that
sprang back, whipping him across the face,
laying his cheek open to the bone. When the
wire passed through his flesh, it wrapped itself around another strand, sending a singing
noise through the fence. Both guards came to
the side of the tower and leaned over to see
what it was. Carelessly, they had left their
weapons behind. Tomanaga quickly made his
decision and two more *phhts* were followed
by dull thuds and shuffling sounds as the men
died. Each one had an extra pupil in his right
eye.

Tomanaga was relieved; it was over and
they didn't have to worry about them anymore. If their luck held, they would be in and
out before anyone noticed the absence of the
men on the tower.

Rossen pushed harder, cutting and tying

the wires back carefully, because this would also be their way out.

Then they were in the compound, lying on their stomachs, watching for the roving guards, the two men who would at odd times check on the prisoner huts. Tomanaga nudged his arm. Coming in from the main gate were two more armed men moving quickly. They went straight to the second hut and entered, coming back out quickly with the smaller of the MIAs. Pushing him along, they headed back out of the compound. Placing the M-14 to his shoulder, Rossen used the scope to bring them into clearer view. Half dragging, half carrying the American, they passed the guard shack and turned across the road heading toward the house with the red tiles.

Pounding his fist into the earth in frustration, Tomanaga hissed, "What now?"

Rossen growled under his breath. "Fuck it! We still take both of them out. Let's get the tall one first, then we'll go for the other."

Pouk witnessed the movement of the MIA to the house and wondered what his friends were going to do about that situation. There were only two possibilities.

Waiting until the roving patrol moved away to the other side of the camp, they hunched

forward and rushed toward the huts, slipping
into the shadows cast by the structures. Tomanaga moved to the side to keep an eye on
the guards, Rossen went for the door. From
his goody bag, he took the heavy metal cutters, wrapped a rag around the chain to muf-
fle the sound, and bore down, increasing the
pressure until the chain broke free with a
small metallic rattle. He froze, looking to both
sides. Still nothing. But things were not going
the way they were supposed to. There had been
a lot of killing and there was sure as hell
going to be some more. Now they had to take
out everyone they could.

Tomanaga slid under the house, invisible in
the mist and the dark. He followed the guards,
keeping under the huts as they passed one
hut, two, three, and finally the fourth hut at
the far end of the camp. If they made a complete circuit they would have to pass the guard
tower where the two dead dinks lay. He
couldn't take a chance on them calling to the
dead men. They had to be stopped before they
got that far.

Sliding into the hut, Rossen closed the door
behind him. His stomach wanted to turn inside out at the sudden stench of urine and
sickness. Quietly, he stood in the center aisle.
On each side were three rows of cells. Stepping to the first, he looked in through the

rusting metal bars. Nothing. Then to the next cell on the opposite side. Nothing. A rustle brought his eyes to the far end. Going to the last cell on the left, he looked through the bars. This was it. His man lay on a straw pallet, his legs pulled to his chest, his arms around them. In the shadows he appeared even more gaunt, eyes sunk back to nothing until he opened them and looked up at the bars. Seeing Rossen standing there, he couldn't tell whether it was a man or perhaps just another nightmare cutting the lock of his door and coming inside after him. He wanted to whimper and crawl farther into the corner of his cell, but he couldn't find the strength. Incredibly, the apparition didn't kick or hurt him. It took him in its arms and spoke words that seemed familiar but he couldn't place them. Then it made a shushing sound, one that he did somehow recall. He had used the same sound to comfort and quiet his children when they were small. Children, his children, they were so small and needed him.

Stepping back into the hallway, Rossen slung the skeletal frame over his shoulder. He might need his hands free. The weight was incredibly light, probably not much more than a hundred pounds on a frame that formerly carried at least two hundred pounds with no problem.

Tomanaga followed the guards as, casually, they made their rounds, talking softly and smoking. They had nothing to fear. Nearing the guard tower, one called up, squinting his eyes to see through the gloom. He started to speak again when his lights went out. Tomanaga let him hold one at the base of the skull. His comrade automatically tried to help his friend to keep him from falling. Bending over, his arms around a dead man, he looked up in time to see a red glow that grew a bit brighter. Tomanaga shot him twice in the forehead. Then he dragged the corpses to where they couldn't be seen by the guards on the other towers if the mist cleared way. Dumping them, he raced back to the hut in time to give Rossen a hand with their prize. Between them they hustled the man back to the wire, having to guide, poke, and push him through the apron. The man simply did not have enough strength to resist them or aid them. Tomanaga went through first; grasping the man's wrists, he pulled as Rossen shoved, and kept the wire from getting entangled in their skin or fatigues. At last they had him free. Rossen hoisted him onto his back and carried him away from the camp as Tomanaga gave cover.

When they reached the edge of the field where the trail started back up the mountain, Rossen set the man down with his back to a tree and did something he wished he didn't have to. He tied the man's hands and gagged his mouth. There was still no slack to be had. Their passage had been witnessed by the Mnong. Leaving the MIA safely secured and out of harm's way, they moved out again. They had to get the last man out of the house with the red tiles. That might be a bit more difficult than the first one had been.

───────────────────────── Twelve

Rossen pulled the Mnong team that had been assigned to the guard tower where they'd offed the two men, taking them with him to join the other two staking out the house.

Crawling on their bellies, they got as close to the house as they could. The windows had rattan shutters through which Rossen could see movement but not enough to make out anything, and they couldn't get close enough to hear what was going on.

Atwood had Carlson on his knees in front of him. Phang observed the proceedings in a detached manner. If Atwood wanted to prove some obscure point by trying to humiliate someone who was so far gone he didn't know it, then it was fine with him. The Americans had already been scheduled for removal. There had been too many stories in the Western press about MIAs in Laos and Vietnam. They were beginning to be a liability.

The wine had soaked deep into Atwood's cells, his face flushed, breathing heavy, every pore open and sweating as he stood over what remained of Major Daniel Carlson. It was good to have him right where he was. To know that if he chose he could kill him right now and there was nothing that could be done to stop him. A good feeling, a strong feeling. He slapped Carlson across the back of his head with the heavy barrel of his 9mm Browning. Carlson pitched forward to the floor, the back of his scalp laid open to the bone. Atwood looked down at the wound. Normally from a scalp wound there was heavy bleeding. Carlson's wound was deep enough, but the blood only came forth in thick bubbles. Atwood began to laugh a bit hysterically at the sight, thinking maybe Carlson's diet for the last few years had lowered his blood pressure.

Stopping, he looked around him. Phang

didn't seem to be too interested in what was going on. Damn it, he wanted an audience!

Stumbling over to the two sleeping women, he kicked them into consciousness. "Get up. Pay attention and learn something, you slope-headed cows."

Phang's eyes narrowed at the remark but he said nothing. Timing was everything. He merely put the remark into his mental book of paybacks.

Atwood dragged the women over to where they could get a proper view of the proceedings.

"Pay attention, sluts. I want you to see how I have trained this piece of shit. This fine officer. This superior human being." He mocked the emaciated and abused form on the floor at his feet.

Grabbing Carlson by the collar of his shirt, he hauled him back to the kneeling position, placing the barrel of the Browning in front of his mouth. Carlson's eyes were dull, nonexpressive, as though what was happening to him didn't really matter. The muscles around his eyes and jaws were slack, his hands grazing the floor palms up.

Atwood didn't like it. It was no fun if the man wasn't aware of what was going on. It spoiled the whole thing.

"Carlson!" He screamed in the man's ear.

"Wake up, you piece of shit. Pay attention to me!"

From deep behind Carlson's eyes, a small spark kindled and grew. The vacuous expression left his eyes, the muscles in his jaws began to work, fingers clenched into fists as his vocal cords strained to find unfamiliar words. He croaked out a thin whisper as he fought to find the strength to raise his head.

"What did you say, you piece of shit? Speak louder, I can't hear you!" Atwood mimicked the cries of his drill instructors during basic training. Carlson tried again and once more Atwood screamed at him, slapping Carlson across the bridge of his nose with the barrel of the pistol.

"I said I can't hear you, you son of a bitch!" Atwood struck once more. The eyes of the women were unable to move away from what was taking place. This was not what they had been sent from Hanoi for; when they returned they would ask for more money in compensation.

Atwood was frantic as bits of froth gathered in the corners of his mouth. Phang observed him with extreme distaste.

"Speak louder, you motherfucker," he screamed at Carlson.

The muscles in Carlson's throat worked, his jaws moved as he tried to find enough saliva to moisten his vocal cords. Searching deep inside, he found enough strength to raise his face and look directly into the eyes of Atwood.

Clearly the words came out. "Atwood, you were always a coward and you are still a coward. Go fuck yourself!"

Stepping back as though he'd been slapped, Atwood couldn't believe it.

"What? What? You dare to talk to me like that?"

Placing the bore of the pistol between Carlson's eyebrows, he shouted, "We'll see who's a coward. Say it again, Major Carlson, sir. Say it again!"

Carlson never moved his eyes from Atwood's.

"Go fuck yourself, punk."

The back of Carlson's head erupted, scattering blood and brain matter over the two stunned whores. The force of the shot knocked Carlson over onto his back. Atwood stood above him, hands trembling in rage. He emptied the magazine into Carlson's face, crying, "You can't speak to me like that. I've got the gun!"

The shots brought the two guards from outside rushing in, weapons at the ready. Atwood screamed at them, "Get out. Get out and back on your posts, you dink sons a bitches!"

They didn't understand the English. Phang waved them back. Confused, they returned to their posts outside.

The gunfire from inside the house had brought everyone on the alert. The surviving guards at the camp, Rossen and his men. When the two guards went inside, Rossen knew they had to move.

"Let's do it!" Rossen got to his knees, ready to move. With Tomanaga at his side, they had just gotten on their feet and were heading across the small patch of open ground when the two guards stepped back out onto the porch. One of them was quick. He reacted, not taking time to think. His AK came to hip level, setting off a long streaming burst of fire at the shadows coming for him. Rossen shot him in the throat. The other guard was saved by the body of the first man, who absorbed all the bullets. Getting off a short burst, the remaining guard rolled backward into the doorway and slammed it shut before Rossen or Tomanaga could reach it.

Phang might be drunk, but he had spent twenty years as a soldier. Rolling from his chair, he had hold of an AK he always kept close by and was under the edge of a window before Atwood's numbed mind could register what was happening.

Cracking the window, he fired off two three-round bursts, not planning on hitting anything but counting on it to slow up whoever was out there until help came from the compound.

Moving back, he grabbed Atwood by the shoulder and pushed him to the window, handing him the AK. "Take this, fool, and shoot something besides prisoners."

To the other Viet guard he commanded, "Cover the door. I'll take the rear of the house."

Entering the back bedroom, Phang opened a closet and removed an RPK light machine gun and an olive-drab belt filled with clips of ammo. Setting up in the rear window, where he had a good field of fire, he waited for help to come.

Phang's shots from the living room had sung over Rossen's head. "Pull back, Tommy, they're on to us." He wanted to just burst in, but that would be stupid now. There was no telling how many men might be inside the house, and the compound was coming alive. Searchlights were coming on. He could hear cries of shock as the dead sentries' bodies were discovered. The shit was getting thick.

Rossen and Tomanaga scuttled back to the high grass for cover. As they did, Phang let loose with a long steady raking fire into the night. Blindly, two of his bullets found one of the Mnong, tearing the right part of his chest open, exposing the lungs to the night mist. The man with him automatically placed the

RPG-7 on his shoulder and with two fingers on the trigger pulled to ignite the friction starter. He aimed at the window where the machine-gun fire had come from. He missed. The round hit to the left and high, blowing a hole through the wall and knocking Phang to his stomach.

When the first RPG round hit, the rest of the Mnong got into the act. Five rockets smashed into the house, two going through windows, the others striking at random. From inside the house, flames began to climb, as clouds of smoke rolled out of the windows and door. From the ceiling, a burning beam fell on the body of Carlson, covering it in flame and smoke. The AK had been knocked from Atwood's hands to fall in a corner. He lay facedown, knocked out from the concussion, blood coming from his ears and mouth, his clothes not on fire but smoldering from the heat as flames crept closer to him.

The two whores lay together, arms around each other, eyes wide as the fire ate at them, turning their ebony hair into blue-flamed pyrotechnic displays. Only the remaining guard was alive and that was just barely. A splinter had laid open his cheek, and bloody teeth showed through the slice in the side of his face. Another had punctured a lung. But he still tried to get to his knees in time to face the two men rushing him. His arms were just not strong enough to raise the incredible weight of his weapon.

When the RPGs hit, Tomanaga and Rossen had turned around, looked at each other, and then without a word, both men ran to the house. Firing from the hip, they hit the now open door, pouring rounds into the remaining guard. Rossen shot him in the throat, nearly ripping head from body as Tommy put five rounds in his chest. They jumped over his body and looked around, trying to see through billowing smoke and growing flames.

Dead women in a corner. But where was the MIA? Tomanaga pointed to a figure lying facedown by the window. The flames had just started eating at the black pajamas and the man's hair and face. Blisters were rising on all exposed skin.

"That's him. I'll carry, you cover." Smothering the smoldering black pajamas as best he could, Rossen put the thin man on his shoulder and fireman-carried him out of the burning building into the clear. Tomanaga came after him, firing short bursts toward the compound where some of the guards had gotten their shit together and finally figured out what was going down. Chest heaving, Rossen carried Atwood away from the house with the red tiles and brightly burning roof to the safety of the dark.

Seng Pouk's Mnong formed a defensive line until Rossen had passed through, then with Tomanaga beside them they fought a delaying action until Rossen had time enough to reach the base of the mountain where his first man was staring at the burning night with wide wondering eyes. Rossen dropped Atwood beside him, set up his M-14, switched on the Starlight, and sighted toward the fires. It was his turn to give some cover now, until Pouk and his men could break contact and help him with the MIAs.

Firing over the heads of Pouk and his men, Rossen let one of the Viets hold one in the belly. He knew that wounded men slowed down the others, especially when they were gut-shot. Men screaming in pain very often reduced the others' desire to get any closer to the source of the agony. Another took one in the chest. The first man had started screaming. Sometimes it took a moment for the shock to wear off and the pain to set in.

The remaining guards drew back, falling to their bellies. They gave out only random and desultory return fire. They were not going after the enemy in the dark, not knowing how many of them there were. They would get help from the garrison down the road. That was the logical thing to do and someone had to make a report and also put out the fire. That did not leave them enough for pursuit in the dark.

Tomanaga joined Rossen with Pouk and his men. Between them they divided up the load, half carrying, half dragging the two MIAs up the dark trail to the top of the hill. Rossen told Pouk, "Be careful with the small guy. He's burned pretty bad." Atwood never moved, still unconscious from the explosion.

Reaching the crest of the hill, they were exhausted. Clothes were glued by sweat to their backs; legs trembled, aching. It was with relief that they set their loads down for a few moments.

Tomanaga went to check on their prizes as Rossen lay down to scope out the way they had just come, checking for any pursuit. Seeing no one, he called Pouk to him. "While we got time, booby-trap that trail."

Even Pouk was too tired and dry-throated to waste words. Nodding, he went and picked out two of his men. Taking grenades and trip wires, they went back down the trail, setting charges not only on the trail but off to the sides where, when the first wire on the tail was tripped, the men behind whoever did it would most likely jump for protection.

* * *

In the house of the red tiles they found Phang. He was lying on his stomach, still stunned by the explosion but suffering no further obvious injury. "Where are they?" It was with relief they heard him speak. Even with his anger it was better to have him make decisions.

Staggering to his feet, Phang directed the men quickly, efficiently. All of the survivors were put to work on the fire. When the bodies were brought out, he had to look at the dead American very closely before ascertaining that it was not Atwood. As for the two burned women, he couldn't have cared less. One of his *trung si*s led him to the guards' quarters. Phang had to shake his head in admiration. Whoever had done this was bold—very bold— and very sure of himself. After checking on the condition of the radio, he sent one of his men by bicycle to the garrison of the 127th Battalion of the PAVN. The message he sent was urgent and would be relayed to his superiors in Hanoi. Within the hour he would have the men and equipment he needed to go after the raiders. He could not let Atwood be taken back alive. The other prisoner was of no great importance, but Atwood had to be stopped.

When the relief forces arrived, they would also bring radio equipment and he would be able to call in what additional forces or equipment he needed. By dawn there would be helicopters in the air as well as forces on the ground coming from every installation around the area for fifty kilometers.

He would have Atwood and the American back, dead or alive, it mattered not; the prisoner, Captain William Vorhees, formerly of the 7th Air Cavalry Division, was going to be killed anyway. The raiders were of even less importance. Without living proof, their claims could be refuted easily, though it would be infinitely more satisfying to have them as his guests for a time, say the rest of their lives!

Now he needed time to think, to clear his mind and put himself in the place of the raiders. What would they be doing? What were their options? Surely, they did not plan to walk out across hundreds of miles of jungle. That meant it had to be by air, and if he had been one of them, he would have the rescue aircraft—whether a helicopter or light plane—on its way as soon as possible. To the east, a rim of lightning lit up the mountains. He looked at the early morning sky. Perhaps the weather would be with him.

"Ten minutes, then we move out. Pouk, see to having a stretcher made. I'll work on his burns. Tomanaga, you try to make contact with Ramasavet. Let's get that damned plane in here so we can get out of this hellhole."

Leaning over the unconscious body of Atwood, Rossen began cutting away the scorched cotton pajamas. The man's face was a mess, eyes swollen, and blisters the size of silver dollars filled with clear fluid threatened to burst at a touch. The hair on the left side of his head was charred nearly to the scalp. Atwood moaned, trying to force open swollen lids as he came back to the real world. Pain ran over him, then fear when he heard the voices in English.

Rossen tried to soothe his fears. "Take it easy, buddy. You're with friends now."

He put three pain pills in Atwood's mouth, then a bit of water to wash them down.

"This will help. We got you out of the camp and we're going to get you back home. Just take it easy. You've been burned a bit, but it doesn't look like you're going to lose anything, so just rest while I put on some ointment and dressings."

Despite his pain, Atwood put it together. They thought he was an MIA and were rescuing him from the Vietnamese! Why? How? Then it came to him. He and Carlson were near the same size and both had been wearing black pajamas. They thought he was Carlson. Did they have his name or know

Carlson's? He had to buy time. Find out more. Best to be silent for a time.

Nodding his head in understanding of Rossen's words, he grabbed the big man's hand and squeezed it.

"You don't have to thank me. This is something that should have been done long ago. Now we're going to put you on a stretcher and carry you out of here. If we can make contact, we'll have a plane in here by noon and you'll be on your way out. It's probably going to hurt you a bit but we can't help that. Okay?"

Atwood nodded again, squeezing the hand as though in gratitude.

Atwood's heart nearly went through his ass when he heard Rossen say, "How's the other one doing? Can he walk or does he have to be carried, too?"

The other one! They got Vorhees out, too! Rolling over to his side, he ignored the pain. There he was, leaning up against a tree with two natives spoon-feeding him something.

Cold fear grabbed him. If Vorhees ever spoke, he'd tell them the truth. Then what would happen to him? Be taken back to the States and tried for treason, publicly humiliated? Life in prison or the death sentence if they found out what he'd been doing for the Viets these last ten years.

Tomanaga called back to Rossen, "I raised Ramasavet. The flight will be over the LZ at 1100 hours and orbit for no more than thirty minutes before it goes back. If we're late they'll try again tomorrow same time at the alternate."

"Did you tell them we had people with us?"

Tomanaga shook his head from side to side. "No! Reception was bad. I did good just to get the signal out for the pickup. But let's get out of here, I don't like it. You know they're going to be on us like ugly on an ape."

Rossen agreed. "All right, let's get them up and moving. We got miles to go!"

The small column formed up: Pouk took point, the MIAs were kept in the middle, two Mnong tribesmen holding on to Vorhees helping him to walk; indeed, they were more than half carrying him. Atwood was carried on a stretcher made from bamboo poles and poncho liner.

He could have walked. His burns looked bad, but none of them were deep enough that they had atrophied any muscle tissue. But if they carried him it would slow them down. Twice he had noticed Vorhees looking at him, eyes confused as if he had the answer to a question he couldn't think of. Each time he looked, Atwood turned his face away, feeling very uneasy. If Vorhees got his mind and mouth working at the same time, it could prove to be very troublesome. He was grateful for the bandages which masked part of his profile.

Tomanaga took a place behind Pouk, and Rossen stayed to the rear. To the east, the sun was just beginning to rise out of the Sea of Tonkin; they had far to go and the daylight was now their enemy. It made traveling easier but it also made them easier to tail. To the north, Rossen heard the flutter of helicopter blades. The dinks were out in force but that was expected. The helicopters were no great threat as long as they were able to stay under the protective canopy of the trees. At the LZ, though, they would be very vulnerable.

Phang had dug through the ruins of his house to find a uniform and boots. They smelled of smoke. He was in a lather by the time the relief force arrived. The Dai Uy in command paid the obvious deference that a captain should to a colonel, as Phang took over command of his troops, spreading them out into a skirmish line. By radio he had been informed that Cambodian units and Pathet Lao forces had also been dispatched to aid in the search. From Attopeu in Laos helicopters had been dispatched to drop troops to the east as blocking forces between the raiders and the Mekong. Cambodia had sent several large detachments north from Siem Pang; these, with the men at Phang's command, would form a pincer which would close on the raiders if they stayed on the ground.

To prevent their exfiltration by air, the air forces of Vietnam, Laos, and Cambodia had been put on alert, with constant flights over the suspect area. Any aircraft not of their origin would be shot down immediately without warning.

Resting under the brilliant colors of a flame tree, the escapees saw a three-bird flight of MIGs heading west at about twenty thousand feet. Ten minutes later they were back. Twice they saw helicopters. One of them was an American Uhlb, now painted kind of shit yellow with a red star; the other was one of those heavy Russian flying tanks, an MI-8 Hip, which carried everything from rockets and infrared to enough armor that it would probably take a 20mm to dent it.

Once, from a ridge, they spotted a detachment of troops. They couldn't make out whether they were Viets or Pathet Lao border guards. Not that it made much difference, they had to be avoided. Rossen began to get the feeling that they were being herded onto a smaller and smaller piece of ground. Another captured

Huey flew by on a zigzag east-to-west course. The neighborhood was definitely getting crowded. From where they were, it was less than ten clicks by air to the LZ. If the plane came in, it wouldn't have much of a chance. The flight of the Huey was taking it directly over the LZ. Too risky in full light.

Pouk, worried, told Tommy, "Warm up the radio and try to raise the field. You have to stop the flight; it'd be stupid to try it now. See if you can reschedule for the alternate for sometime tonight. It'll take us at least eight more hours to get there."

Tomanaga helped the Mnong tribesman with the radio to get it off his back, then sent him up a tree to set up the jungle antenna.

Tomanaga tried the radio for ten minutes. "I can't raise shit on this thing. All I get is static. Think maybe the Viets might be doing some jamming?"

Shrugging his shoulders wearily, Rossen said, "Hell, I don't know. But if you can't raise them, then we got to go on to the LZ. Maybe we'll get lucky."

Under his breath, Tomanaga swore softly, "I wouldn't give any odds on it."

Thirteen

Phang stayed to the road, taking the Zis jeep the Dai Uy had brought with him from the garrison. By radio, he directed the hunt. Overhead, helicopters and planes joined in the search. It was most probable they would try to get out by air and there were only so many places available for an aircraft to set down. A helicopter was unlikely. Too slow, too easy to spot, and the distance back to the Thai frontier too great—over 150 kilometers. Air patrols were covering the approaches; considering the enemy's maximum possible rate of movement, it would not be very difficult to cover the area by air. If they stayed to the earth, then his patrols would push them up the banks of the Kong River and again he would have them.

Tomanaga kept watch as Rossen tried to talk to the MIAs.

Patting the tall man on his shoulder gently, he asked, "What's your name? Can you tell me?"

Vorhees tried to get his tongue to form words, but it felt too large, uncontrollable.

"Tommy, I don't like the way this man looks. We got to get him out of here soon or I don't think he'll make it."

The captain's skin was yellow, the color of old parchment. Rossen took two fingers and pulled a piece of skin on the back of his hand. It stayed up, the pinch marks showing clearly. The man was severely dehydrated and feverish. No telling what bugs had settled in his system.

"Okay, buddy, I've got something that might help." As he would have handled a small, ill child, he rolled Vorhees over onto his stomach and pulled down his trousers. The bare buttocks were sunken in, the hip sockets easily seen. Rossen searched for the fleshiest part to give him an injection of 600 units of penicillin. He wished he were able to set up an IV to get some fluids back into the man's veins before they completely collapsed.

Setting his back up against the bole of a tree, the man motioned for Rossen to come closer to his mouth. Vorhees' throat strained with the effort as he hissed out something.

Tomanaga leaned over to them. "Did he say something?"

Rossen nodded, smiling. "Yeah, we got a name. Bill Vorhees, right?"

The skeleton's lips formed a small smile, the first in over ten years, and he nodded his head up and down once, then quit as if the effort was just too great.

Standing up, Rossen felt good. He had made progress; at least he had a name now. He started to ask Vorhees what the other man's name was, but decided it could wait—they still had a couple of clicks to go to the LZ. They didn't want to be late.

Atwood had played dumb all the way; when Rossen had gotten the name from Vorhees his heart nearly dropped out of his ass again. So far he'd been lucky, but he had to do something. If Vorhees' mind cleared any more, he would be certain to expose him. Now they were less than an hour from the LZ; once there, if the plane got them, he was finished.

Pouk was again on point, clearing away the

worst of the brush with a smooth practiced swing of his native short sword. They were leaving the hills, going down into a verdant valley, nothing but jungle until they reached a place where the valley widened. There a riverbed was exposed during the dry season. The bank of the river was their LZ. Going down the hill, Atwood shifted his body, falling out of the stretcher and rolling. The pain was excruciating as scabs were torn open. He cried out as thorn vines ripped at the tender wounded flesh. It took nearly ten minutes to get him back up the hill and onto his stretcher. Ten whole minutes. The price he paid in pain was small if it served its purpose.

"Push it, Pouk, we're running late. If we're not there, the plane's not going to set down and I don't blame him. Push it."

Pouk did push harder, and the Mnong picked up the pace. Atwood thought they were going to rattle his bones out of his skin as they half trotted on to the valley floor. Rossen had handed Tomanaga his weapon and put Vorhees on his back, and began trotting. Time was not good. If the plane was able to get in and they missed it, they would have to march through the night to the next rendezvous. Another Hip flew over to the north side of the valley rim. They kept to the cover of the trees, hoping the infrared detectors weren't scanning in their direction. It passed on.

Pouk went on ahead to check out the LZ as the rest struggled after him. Vorhees seemed to be gaining a bit in strength. Perhaps, Rossen thought, it was because he was gradually realizing what had taken place. He hoped so. It would make things easier for him.

They caught up to Pouk where a clump of brush and bamboo interspaced with breadfruit trees lined the edge of the strip where the plane was to set down. Grateful, they lay their burdens down.

"Tommy, try the radio again." Rossen checked his watch. "If he's on time we got about ten minutes left."

Then, looking around the area, he ordered Pouk, "Set out some men. We've come too far to get sloppy now."

"*Xa phai*, Phü Nhām." Three of the Mnong went out, disappearing into the bush.

Tomanaga labored over the radio; finally, in frustration, he pounded the top of it with his clawed fist.

"I can't get nothing on the son of a bitch. Nothing but static and garbage. The Viets must be jamming." Slumping wearily by the radio, he propped his head on the side of his hand. "I never thought they would get their act together this fast. Shit, they've got everything that can walk, fly, or crawl out after us, and they did it fast."

Rossen knew he was right. The operation was beginning to sour. "I know, but we don't have any choice right now. In eight minutes we'll know more. Now, help me with Vorhees and the other one. I still don't know his name. He hasn't said a word, just groans a lot."

They shared water with the two men, Tomanaga giving Vorhees a chocolate bar to suck on. The ex-POW looked at the candy, then at Tomanaga, and shied away, afraid to put the candy in his mouth. His eyes withdrew from the real world again.

Tomanaga stood up, confused. "What did I do?"

"I think he just noticed that you're an Oriental. Here, I'll do it."

Sitting by the man, he broke off a small square of chocolate, and gently pressed it between Vorhees' lips, speaking softly, encouragingly.

"It's all right. We're all friends here. No one is going to hurt you." Pointing over to Atwood on his stretcher, he added, "See, we even have your buddy with us. We're taking you both out."

Vorhees' eyes followed the pointing finger. A whimper started deep in his gut and broke as sobs on the surface when the man on the stretcher turned a bit to his side, exposing his face. The whimpers grew louder as the piece of unchewed and untasted chocolate melted on his lips, running thick and brown down his chin to his neck. His cracked lips formed silent words, "Help. Help me." He covered his eyes with his hands and wept, repeating over and over, "Help me."

Rossen put his arm around the thin man's shoulders. "We will help you. We are helping you. Take it easy, everything's all right."

The crackling from the radio receiver cleared, breaking in and out. "You fucking guys want to get out of here or not?"

All interest in the MIAs was put aside as Rossen and Tomanaga leaned over the radio. Hitting the talk switch, Tomanaga answered, "Roger that, Mother Goose. We read you three by three. We are on-site. Do you Roger? Over."

"Roger that. But what's the Mother Goose shit? Ain't no one up here but us drunks. By the way, how's the wind down there?"

"No wind. Come on in, we're ready to go. We have two more to exit with us. Do you Roger? Over."

"Right on, Papa San. Two more to go. I'm coming down."

"Go get Pouk and the others, Tommy. We're going home." Vorhees' eyes sparkled at the words "going home"; then he looked at Atwood and the glow faded.

Tomanaga yelled out, "I can hear it. It's coming." From his pack Rossen took a white-smoke grenade, pulled the pin, and tossed it onto what was to be their runway. The cloud rose almost straight up, a guidepost for their ride out of the green hell.

Tomanaga pointed to the west. "There she is!" The Beech was coming just over the far end of the valley, flaps down, throttle back, coming dead on. From the bush, the Mnong stood at the sides and cheered. The Beech was down to less than ninety miles an hour and settling nicely as Tomanaga and Rossen hauled the MIAs over to the end of the strip.

"No!" Pouk screamed out. The plane disintegrated in a ball of flame fifty feet off the ground. The explosion knocked him and Tomanaga on their backs. Then the other sound came to them, heavy automatic fire followed by heavier thumps as rockets bracketed the strip.

Rolling over, Rossen saw what it was. One of the Russian Hip-8 armored choppers was coming at them from the north side of the valley.

"Oh, shit!" Another long burst of fire from the Hip's nose machine guns took one of the Mnong out. Throwing his rifle to his shoulder,

Rossen pulled off five rounds on full auto, hitting the Plexiglas shield in front of the pilot. Though the rounds didn't get him, it shook the pilot bad enough that his reflexes took over. The Hip swerved off to the side.

"Let's go. Pouk, move it out back to the trees."

Tomanaga and Pouk grabbed Vorhees. Rossen pulled Atwood up off his stretcher and onto his shoulders. Skin cracked open, forcing a cry of pain from his lips. Rossen followed after Tomanaga and Pouk. Behind him came the other Mnong. Relieved, they made it to the relative security of the trees, but there was no time to rest. From the Hip came a barrage of rockets, several exploding in the treetops, sending down splinters of wood and metal in a shower over the fleeing men. Random machine-gun fire also came close as they pushed their way deeper into the foliage.

Now that they had been spotted, ground troops would be coming. They needed to find a place to hole up and rest. If they hadn't had the two MIAs with them . . .

Not only the tropic sun and jungle but his overworking inner furnace turned Rossen's environment into a living sweatbox. The extra weight of Atwood on his back, along with that of his pack, made every step a major effort.

He had to lock his mind down, taking one step at a time, each one a victory, a goal. Even the forest was silent for a change. He had blocked the cries of tree frogs, birds, and monkeys in the branches overhead, ignoring everything but the next step. Time lost relevance; he didn't know how far they had come when his face hit the spongy earth. A horned beetle the size of his thumb scooted past his nose to disappear under a pile of decaying humus.

Atwood screamed when he fell from Rossen's shoulders. Landing on his back, the force of the fall and twisting of his body tore open a burn scab the size of his two hands, exposing raw red meat.

Gulping air through a dry throat, Rossen croaked out, "Sorry. Sorry."

His fall brought them all to a halt. The Mnong didn't sit, they leaned against trees, eyes on the way they had come. Tomanaga sat cross-legged by Rossen after seeing that Vorhees and Atwood were settled down.

"How far did we come, Tommy?"

"We been running about an hour and a half. In this terrain I figure that we made maybe four miles topside." Eyeing his exhausted friend, he said, "Why didn't you give your man to me? I asked you three times but you just kept on going. You nuts or something?"

"I didn't hear you. Guess I went into a fade."

Tomanaga knew what he meant.

"What now, boss? Cross-country run?"

Rolling over to his back, Rossen took a pull from his canteen. "That's it. There won't be another aircraft coming in for us. We're on our own. Time for some serious E&E."

Escape and evasion. They had done that before, but never having to travel so far with two sick men.

"Right. I'll talk to Pouk and fill him in. See what he thinks about the best way out from here."

Rolling back over to his stomach, Rossen closed his eyes. "Yeah, you do that. We'll crash here for fifteen minutes, then move out. I want to find somewhere to hole up for the night before it gets too dark."

Atwood felt a shudder of relief run through him. There wasn't going to be another plane or helicopter. He still had a chance. Eyeing Vorhees, he knew what had to be done if he was to survive, and it had to be done fast. Every second's delay put him in more danger of discovery. He turned his attention to the Mnong and the Americans—what were their names, Rossen and Tomanaga? Yeah, that was it—he had to do everything he could to slow them up until Cao Lam Phang caught up to them. That he would was certain. He knew that

Phang was making every possible effort to find them. It was his ass, too, if he didn't.

From his jeep, Phang listened to the report of the Hip-8 pilot. They had been located, and an unidentified aircraft had been shot down. The raiders were on the ground, heading south.

Good, very good. He gave his R/T operator instructions to contact all the search parties and give them the raiders' last known location. He could begin to tighten the strings of his net. He had over one thousand men on the job. *He would have them!* From Hanoi he had received a message of encouragement, salted with a sincere regret for what might take place if Atwood was not recovered.

Rossen hoped that Harding, their drunken pilot, had gone to a heaven made in the image of a distillery.

Fourteen

Vorhees had started to lose ground again. He just didn't have the reserves of strength to call on. Within two hours of breaking contact with the Hip, he had begun to shiver and shake, his skin growing clammy and pale, eyes dilating. It was back to piggy-back for him. The Americans rotated and the Mnong took turns carrying the gaunt figure.

Atwood dragged his feet at every turn, scuffing the earth, bending leaves, breaking branches where he could. He had had to give Rossen his name, not knowing if Vorhees had done it already. He didn't want to be caught in any kind of lie this early. He had noticed the Jap watching him. There was a touch of suspicion behind the brown orbs that he didn't like. It was best now to try and go along with them, to show that he was on their side and wanted nothing more in life than to get away. The scuff marks and broken branches were done only when he was certain that he would not be seen doing them.

As near as Seng Pouk could figure it, they were somewhere northwest of Siem Pang in Cambodia and east of the Kong River in Laos when they entered a range of low trees and new growth. The new growth and young trees were the results of a Viet sweep a couple of years earlier in pursuit of the Khmer Rouge. Orientals often have a practical approach to things. If people didn't have cover or food, they were easier to find and control. The fires they set to burn out croplands and villages were almost as efficient as the American use of Agent Orange.

Passing the barren region, the rescue party came off a plateau and down into a narrow valley. They entered a place of dark shadows, where trees hung with heavy leaves, and arm-thick tendrils hung from their tops to the soft earth. Here the sun seldom reached the earth.

Rossen sighted with his compass, trying to maintain as straight a line of march as possible and knowing it was futile. The undergrowth was simply too thick; it tripped and tore at them, forcing them to go its way in spite of their curses. It would have been easier if Rossen had permitted them to use their machetes to clear a path, but that was forbidden. Cut marks would mark their trail for the enemy. There would be no cutting—they had to just bend and twist with the jungle. Where it was too thick to go through or under they would go around.

The MIAs weren't much help, but at least Vorhees seemed to be getting a bit better and was able to walk some without help. The other one definitely wasn't much fucking help. The man held them back, complaining of his burns and wounds. Rossen had forced him to his feet to walk. Tomanaga had checked him over, the burns hadn't hurt his legs. Every step he took on his own saved that much of their strength. There was something about him that Rossen didn't like. He couldn't put his finger on it, just something.

Pouk was on point when he called back to them. "Phü Nhãm, come here!"

Rossen scuttled forward, nearly losing an eye to a whipping vine with thorns on it the size of knitting needles.

Crouching by Pouk, he peered through the undergrowth, his eyes following Pouk's pointing finger.

"No shit!"

There, in an emerald glade covered with the growth of centuries, faces peered back at him stoically, unconcerned, as they had been since the days when the great temple city of Angkor Wat had been built.

Behind the weathered statue of an inscrutable Buddha he made out the forms of buildings covered with detritus. From them, trees reached up eighty feet, their roots embedded in the cracks between the stones and bricks. The temples dripped with lush growth and vines; it was almost a waterfall of green. From the sky they would be invisible; even on the deck, you would have to get within fifty yards to make them out. He wondered how long it had been since the last man had set foot here.

Behind him, the rest of the small column filed into the glade, heads tilted back, staring in awe at the desolate, lonely remains of an empire long turned to dust.

From the east came heavy earth-trembling rumbles resembling that of a distant artillery barrage.

Pouk didn't look up; he knew by smelling the air.

"It will rain this night. A big rain, then it will pass before dawn."

Tomanaga sniffed the air. It tasted cooler. "He's right." Looking at the two MIAs, he went on, "Maybe we ought to hole up here. Traveling at night in the rain won't do either one of them much good. And if the dinks do catch up to us, at least we'll have some walls to fight from."

Rossen knew he was right. As weak as they were, a night in the jungle with a storm could be too much for them. Everyone needed some rest and food.

"Okay, Tommy, we'll stay here." He pointed to the temples. "Pouk, check 'em out. We're going to hole up here for the night. If it's a good storm Charlie will have to do the same."

"*Xa phai*, Phü Nhãm, as you wish." Taking two men, Pouk moved into the larger of the two main temples. Taking his time, he moved slowly, eyes wary for the slither of a serpentine body. It was well known that cobras and kraits loved to live in the ancient stones of these places.

Tomanaga dropped his pack, keeping only his weapon and ammo. "Rossen, I'm going to backtrack a ways. I'll be back in an hour. Let Pouk and the others know so they don't get trigger-happy."

"Good thinking. You go ahead, I'll hold

things down here. When the rains come we'll even be able to get some hot chow. That'll do us all some good."

"Right. See you in an hour."

Tomanaga disappeared back down the trail, the tiger-stripe pattern of his fatigues blending, then vanishing into the jungle's thousand shades of green.

Atwood didn't like the Jap going back into the bush. He liked even less the way Vorhees' eyes would light up from time to time, and his lips would try to form words. He knew that if those words ever came out he was going to be in a world of shit.

Pouk came back out from the first temple. In his hand he held a torch he'd made of dried wood and palm fronds. Quickly, he ran over to the second ruin, poking his head inside under the linteled doors. He was in there for less than five seconds and was back out, face pale, hands shaking. He set the torch down, the butt in a crack between the temple stones.

"Rats, Phü Nhãm. Thousands of rats in that place. We go into the first one. It is best."

His reasoning was good enough for Rossen. Just the idea of a dark place filled with rats was more than enough to make him go along with Pouk's judgment. The thought passed him quickly that if the other temple didn't have rats there must be a reason.

"Right, Pouk. Let's move everybody in, drop our gear, then put out some security and watch for Tommy. He went backtracking and will be returning in about an hour."

"Okay." With the help of the Mnong he moved Vorhees and Atwood into the doorway of the temple. He set two men as sentries, picked up his torch, and went back into the ruins with the Phü Nhām.

Rossen was hesitant at first. Somehow it didn't seem right that he should be setting foot in a place where priests and kings had paid homage to their gods. The ruins still had an aura of stateliness and mystery. Faces watched him from the walls. Carvings of dancers and warriors captured for eternity in frozen movement.

Pouk moved deeper into the ruin, waving his torch to burn away cobwebs which hung as gossamer drapes to which the dust of ages clung in moving clots as air crept into the interior chambers.

By the glow of Pouk's torch, Rossen could see a figure rising above them at the rear of the chamber. Legs crossed, hands lying palms up on his thighs in the lotus position, a Buddha gazed down on them with heavy lidded eyes, face eternally peaceful, not questioning the arrival of these new ones who sought shelter in his house. He welcomed all, benign, calm. To the stone image of the holy one, time was as nothing, and soon these intruders would also pass away into the mists of an antiquity yet to come.

The Mnong cleared a place on the floor, sweeping it semiclean with palm fronds they had gathered at the entrance. Gently, they helped Vorhees and Atwood to lie down, giving up their packs for pillows. Then they, too, went to explore, climbing around, over, and through fallen stones into antechambers and back out. Once this was done, each of them went to sit cross-legged in front of the Buddha. Bowing their heads to touch the floor, they honored the ancient figure with new prayers, then each moved to where he could see the outside, weapon at the ready.

Watching them, Rossen recalled once long ago when he and Tomanaga had been on a ride into Cambodia. They had contacted Charlie in a clearing where several rows of Buddhas sat in a line. There among the manifestations of the Holy One they had fought and killed. When it was over, twenty-three men, Viets and Americans, lay dead. The Buddhas had looked down on the dead with the same calm expression, as if to say it makes no difference if East and West meet and die. I shall continue for I am not of this madness.

Finding a spot on a ledge near the entrance,

he set his own pack down. Taking a dry, clean rag, he worked on his weapon, putting just a touch of oil on the action of the receiver group. *God, I am getting old. Not long ago thoughts like that would never have entered my mind. Maybe when this is over I'll call it quits. There's got to be something else I can do. Isn't there?*

Vorhees lay beside Atwood, his body shaking, eyes closed, the lids already crusting with dry, yellowed pus. Atwood watched him carefully; not moving, he pretended to sleep, even though the pain of his burns was excruciating. The less he drew attention to himself, the better.

From the entrance, one of the sentries hissed, motioning for Rossen to come over to him.

Staying to the shadows, Rossen looked out. Tomanaga was just entering what had once been the courtyard. From his body movement, Rossen knew that he hadn't seen anything or anyone. He moved easily, not looking back, his weapon at the ready but casual, nothing tense except, perhaps, a bit of stiffness to his neck and spine. Overhead, the sky was darkening rapidly; from the east, more lightning crackled, followed by rolling thunder coming closer to them. A crack of lightning hit the plateau behind Tomanaga; from the count, Rossen figured it was three clicks away.

Tommy climbed up the short flight of stairs to stand beside Rossen.

"What's the score, Tommy?"

Undecided, Tomanaga shook his head. "I don't know. There's a lot of sign back on the trail to show where we passed. Too much sign."

"Well, we are hauling some dead weight with us." He looked up to the sky, where heavy black clouds were gathering. "Anyway, the storm will cover most of our sign. Charlie will have a tougher time picking up our trail after tonight."

Still not satisfied, Tomanaga shook his head, scratched his ass with his claw. "Like you say."

Rossen knew he wasn't satisfied, but there was nothing you could put your finger on. Hauling two weak and sick men with them, it wasn't too difficult to understand if they left something other than a sterile trail.

"Go on in and sit down. When the rain starts I'll let Pouk build a fire."

"Okay, I'm bushed. You know, I didn't really plan on having to walk out of this son of a bitch."

Tomanaga found a place across from the MIAs. Leaning his back up against the wall, he sat watching them. Vorhees didn't look good at all. Fever. Probably a combination of a half-dozen things, from malaria to dengue and God knows what else, maybe even leptospirosis. The first medication had seemed to help for a while, but even with repeated doses of penicillin and primaquine, Bill Vorhees was losing ground. Maybe he was just worn out.

Still at the entrance, Rossen saw the first fat drops of rain strike the courtyard, bouncing small puffs of dust from hand-hewn flagstones. Then the rains came as they only can in the tropics. The sky opened and let loose. This was not rain as it was known in the States.

This was a deluge where a man could drown if he looked up, where the skyflood beat so hard that it could knock animals to their knees. And with the rains came the winds whipping the storm into a blinding sheet. In less than twenty seconds rivulets were rushing together, washing over the flagstones ankle-deep, and rising until they reached the edge of the courtyard, draining off onto lower ground to run until they reached the stream which was already flowing brown. Froth was whipped up to ride on the surface of the waters as the valley walls fed the stream, turning it into a raging torrent which would pass as quickly as it had come. In this land, nature seldom did anything in a moderate manner. Everything was accented.

The two men Pouk had put on guard duty came rushing in, gasping for air. Rossen waved them on. None would travel this night, and if they did they would be going blind. Until the rain eased, there wasn't any sense in leaving anyone outside.

In the center of the chamber, Pouk had started a fire, using dried vines and debris which he gathered from inside the temple to feed the flames.

Rossen pulled back into the interior, drawn by the welcome glow of the fire. There was something about a campfire which made it a welcome place. Perhaps it was a primal thing going back through the eons to a time when fire was something which kept the evils of the night at bay. He warmed his hands by the welcoming glow, which sank into his flesh. It was good.

One by one the Mnong settled, each finding a place to lie down. This was a good time, a time to rest. Wrapping the blankets about them, they quickly fell into an untroubled sleep.

Rossen looked around. Two of the Mnong were still on watch, one at the entrance, another who had climbed up a series of ledges to where he could look out through an opening in the temple dome. They could see nothing outside because of the torrent and dark which had settled on the valley. But they were there.

Weariness hit him in a rush. Suddenly, his muscles felt very heavy, very tired. Sighing, he sat down at the edge of the campfire's glow. Removing his boots, he placed his feet toward the fire, luxuriating in the sensuous pleasure the fire gave him. Over his shoulder he heard a small snore. Tomanaga had gone to sleep sitting up, arms crossed over his chest, his steel claw glowing red and gold reflecting the colors of the flames. Vorhees and Atwood were also asleep.

Pouk had lain down on the altar in front of the statue of Buddha. Head on his arms, he too slept deep. Rossen wasn't aware of when his own eyes closed, it just became quiet, pleasant. He slept a dreamless sleep. Deep, heavy.

All slept deep. Even those by the temple entrance and at watch from the dome slipped off. All except Atwood, and it had taken all of his will to stay awake. Vorhees was only an arm's distance away, mumbling, beads of sweat forcing their way out of every fevered pore. Atwood edged closer to him. One of his burns broke open, oozing serous fluid from the wound. Straining to control his breathing as it roared in his own ears, he was surprised that the sound of it didn't awaken any of the sleeping men.

Vorhees' eyes opened a crack, trying to focus through pus-filled lids. He saw the figure beside him coming closer as though in a haze, indistinct, spectral. He blinked; tear ducts flowed, washing the lenses clear of the fog. The face near his own took a second to register.

His lips formed the word "you" accusingly. "You," he hissed, barely audibly, "Atwood, you trait . . ." He never finished the word. Atwood's thumbs had reached deep into the sides of his neck. Not touching the esophagus, Atwood applied pressure only on the carotid arteries, stopping the flow of blood to Vorhees' brain. His palms spread smoothly, tightening the skin over the throat; there would be no sign of strangulation, no bruise or broken cartilage on the throat. Only a slight discoloration on the thick muscle directly below the hinge of the jaw.

Darkness took the captain as Atwood applied pressure. Not blinking, he gazed calmly into the eyes of his killer. Not accusing, not even surprised. It was as if everything was expected, normal. Nothing to be concerned about.

Atwood increased the pressure, his thumbs molding to the conformation of the throat. It would have been quicker, easier, to have just strangled him, but it would have left more physical evidence. This way there would be little sign; only a trained eye could possibly notice the discoloration and with Vorhees' already yellowish complexion there was little likelihood that anyone would think anything other than that the already weakened man had simply died in his sleep. Atwood sweated copiously with the effort. To kill the man this way took a minimum of five minutes; he gave him eight by a mental count. When he finally released his victim to slide back over to his original position, he was totally exhausted. Arms and fingers trembled from the strain. But it was done. He was safe now. There was no one to tell of what he had done even if they managed to get him into Thailand. He was safe. Safe!

Then he slept, too.

Comfortable, secure in his safety.

Fifteen

"Wake up!" Tomanaga shook Rossen's shoulder. "C'mon, wake up!"

Rossen's eyes jerked open. "What is it? Charlies?"

"No. Vorhees is dead."

Getting to his feet, Rossen looked around. Everyone was asleep, Pouk still at the foot of the Buddha, the rest of the Mnong where they had first lain down. Looking to the entrance, he saw the man on guard there was also out. "Tomanaga, check out the other guard."

He stepped over Atwood, who had a peaceful look to his face as he slept. Kneeling beside the still body, he took the thin wrist, feeling for a pulse. Nothing. Then fingers to the side of his throat for the carotid. Still nothing. The body was warm, he hadn't been dead very long. In the glow of the fire the man looked quite calm. His pain and nightmares were behind him.

Now they had one. One man to get out. Already the price had been high, counting the dead among the Mnong, and it wasn't over. There would very likely be more dead before this journey was ended. Standing up, he looked down. Vorhees seemed to be even smaller, more frail. What was there about death that diminished man? When the life force or soul, whatever, departed, something went out with it. Was it what made man a living being?

Tomanaga, moving up behind him with a blanket to cover the corpse, broke his train of thought. He was grateful for it. Too many questions came to him as he got older.

Moving away with Tomanaga, he asked, "What do you think he died of? Fever?"

Tomanaga shook his head. "I don't know. Maybe. I checked him over pretty close before waking you, but I just don't know." Leaning against the wall, he rubbed his eyes with his good hand. "There are just some things I don't like. You've felt it, too. I can't put my finger on it because none of it makes any sense. It just doesn't make any sense."

Rossen leaned beside him, lighting up a smoke. "I know what you mean. I've got the same feeling." Taking a long drag, he blew out. "Well, at any rate we still have one alive and he's getting better. Let's just concentrate on the job and get his ass and ours out of this fucking place."

Tomanaga agreed, but the worry around the corners of his eyes refused to go away.

Another crack of thunder shook the temple, knocking dust from the vaulted ceilings to float over the interior in fine mist.

Rossen picked up his rifle. "You go and get some more sleep. I'll take a stand on watch." Leaving Tomanaga, he went out the entrance, tapped the Mnong on his shoulder, and pointed back inside.

Once alone, he faced out to the storm. Winds and rains obliterated everything. Only during the flashes of lightning could he see the trees being bent nearly double as the storm screamed about them. Debris and branches torn from the trunks of trees a thousand years old, and the thickness of a man's thigh, flew past. The wind was cold, chilling his body and face, but it felt good. When the storm passed, the day would turn into a sweltering oven as the sun rose. It was 0523 hours. Dawn would be coming in a couple of hours. Dawn, and then what? They had a long way to go and time was not on their side. Every hour could bring them closer to death. Every villager they saw or that saw them could turn them in. He knew patrols were out watching the passes and trails which led to Thailand.

Rossen was still at the entrance when the sun rose over the rim of the green cliffs surrounding them. With the passing of the storm there was now only mist rising in shimmering waves into the tops of the trees, floating in the low spots, moving gently, softly ethereal.

Inside he could hear Tommy giving Pouk orders to bury Vorhees and get ready to move out.

Cao Lam Phang was ready, too. He had spent a miserable night in a hut he had requisitioned from some peasant family, forcing them outside so he would not have to endure the smell of their bodies in the closeness of the already pungent hut. His men took what shelter they could under trees or by wrapping their bodies in shelter halves or blankets. They did not concern him. What did was that after the rains the trail could be very difficult to pick up. With grudging admiration he had to give Atwood credit.

He had left them enough sign that at least they knew the general direction the raiders were taking. With the dawn, the chase would begin again. Calling his RTO to him, he sent messages to all units. They were to begin to tighten their circle and converge at the junction of the rivers. Especially, they were to be on the alert for signs of the raiders' passage and to question all villagers they encountered.

From Phnom Penh in Cambodia and Attopeu in Laos, helicopters and light aircraft were being readied on their runways to participate in the search.

Stepping out to the porch and down the steps leading from the hut to the spongy earth, he breathed deep. He still had time on his side. At a good rate of march, with no problems, it would take his quarry at least four to five more days to reach the Thai border. Five days. He would have them before then.

"Five days' march, Tommy. If we don't run into any major problems and Atwood doesn't slow us up anymore, we'll be across the Mekong into Thailand."

Atwood was up, shuffling about, trying to find a place where he could take a leak in private. When he had eased the pressure on his bladder, Rossen cornered him, speaking sympathetically. "I'm sorry about your buddy, lasting this long and being so close to getting out then buying it."

Atwood picked his words carefully and the manner of his saying them. He had to keep up his appearance of being weaker than he really was, to put his mind into that of a POW.

Letting his face take on a slack, slightly uncomprehending expression, he responded, "What?"

"He's dead, Vorhees is dead. Do you understand?"

Atwood faced Rossen, careful to avoid direct contact with the sniper's eyes. "Dead?"

A tear found its way to Atwood's eye. He had always thought he would have made a consummate actor.

Careful not to overplay his role, he sat down in the dust of the temple. Sitting there, legs crossed, he lowered his head, eyes to the dust, repeating, "Dead. Dead. All dead."

Rossen felt a deep cold in his soul. The tragedy. It wasn't like war, this was something of the spirit. God knows what the poor devil had been put through. The years of half starving, torture, brainwashing. Now, when there were just two of them left to help each other, to lean on, when they were this close to escaping, one dies.

"Shit!" Rossen stomped away. "The whole world is shit!"

Tomanaga watched the scenario with a cynical eye. Shaking his head, he went outside with Pouk to where the Mnong had dug a grave. It would go unmarked; even now they could do nothing that would give the enemy any information about them. But this was a good place. It had a feeling of peace to it and the Lord Buddha would watch over the spirit and physical remains until he, too, crumbled back into the dust of eternity.

When the body was covered, they gathered around the site, each man's thoughts to himself. Atwood stood with stooped, weary shoulders, shaking slightly as if in great exhaustion of spirit. Tomanaga did nothing, just watched everyone. He had taken one last look at the body in the full light before it was placed into the rich earth.

Rossen had them camouflage the grave, removing all signs of it, smoothing away the mound and transplanting some ferns and elephant ears to conceal it further.

"Let's move it out!"

Pouk took point again; he didn't need a compass to know the directions of the wind and sky. He could feel it in his bones, even on the darkest and stormiest of nights. He knew which way they had to go. Once more the small column formed up, one of the Mnong aiding Atwood.

Into the mist they moved, feet sinking ankle-deep in the soaked earth. In less than five minutes they were soaked as badly as if they'd been out in the rain. The humidity was incredible—by midday the jungle would make a Turkish bath seem frigid.

From the valley, they followed a thin trail running alongside the stream until it branched sharply to the south. Limestone cliffs broke through the green, shrouded in mist.

"Well, I guess it's time to head up and out." Reaching the top was easier said than done. Every step up was a major achievement. Wet leaves, loose earth, tripping, trailing vines, and falling rocks mocked every movement. By the time they reached the top, the sun was high in the sky. Looking below, the way they had come was a world belonging to the primal past. Rossen wouldn't have been surprised to see a tyrannosaur, or a pterodactyl flying through the mist.

At the top they took a break; all of them needed it. Rice balls prepared the night before were handed around. Plain rice spiced with a touch of *nouc mam* sauce and water was their meal for the day. Only Atwood was given as much as he wanted; it was important to build up the man's strength for the days ahead.

Tomanaga had taken up a spot behind

Atwood and his Mnong helper along the route. This time there were few marks left on their trail.

Standing, Rossen looked around him. Each direction was the same. Green mountains rising above mist-laden valleys stretched in all directions. To the east, out of sight, was freedom and safety. Five days. Five days' march. Not so bad—he and Tomanaga had done a lot more in their time and the Mnong certainly had, too. The difference was that then they didn't have aircraft, helicopters, and enemy troops all on their ass at the same time.

There were no friendlies here to take refuge with. Villagers were not to be trusted. Not that all of them supported the Viets; it was just safer. All it took was one collaborator and they'd have their balls in their mouths before nightfall.

Staying to the treeline, and away from the cleared areas or fields, they headed east. The Mnong kept changing places with each other to help with Atwood. He couldn't be allowed to slow them up; when he tired, or paused or stumbled, a brown stringy arm was there to help him back up, urging him on.

Coming off the plateau, they entered a wide valley where signs of fields long unused were in evidence. Following a red-clay trail, they passed small groves of banana trees growing wild, untended.

Rossen lay on his belly, focusing his glasses on the village. It was built, as most were, along the banks of a small river. In his glasses, the village appeared to be deserted. No sign of life. No smell of smoke on the air. Most of the hooches were falling apart. Thatched roofs were falling in and there were no animals—dogs or pigs—wandering about. It was dead.

"Okay, Pouk, we'll go in."

To bypass the village they would have to go four or five clicks around, and here he knew there was a place to ford the river. Right at the edge of the village, water rippled, telling him it was shallow. Where the next crossing was he didn't know—it could be a hundred miles if the rains last night had done their job.

Leaving Atwood with one of the Mnong, they spread out into a skirmishing line and advanced on the village.

It was dead. Scattered about were the skeletons of whoever the people were that had lived here. Scraps of clothing faded by sun and rain stuck to white stark rib cages and fluttered gently with the breeze coming in from the highlands.

They spread out, weapons at the ready, to check the rest of the village. In every hut, along each path, it was the same. Men, women, children—all had been killed. Most of the bodies were in the open, what remained of them. The animals had been at them. Some lay on the porches of the long houses or thin pallets inside.

What had killed most of them he couldn't tell. Some of them had bullet holes in the backs of their heads and their wrists were still tied together with pieces of baling wire. Others showed no sign of violence.

Not all of the dead were human. The smaller bones of dogs lay about; some of these still had scraps of fur hanging to thin bones, lips drawn back in eternal snarls.

"What do you think happened here, Pouk?"

Looking to the sky where small bands of white clouds drifted, the little man replied, "The yellow rain fell here, then the Viet Minh soldiers came and killed those who were still alive." He moved about the clearing, touching, looking. "Yes, it is clear. That is what happened."

Rossen had no reason to doubt him. It made sense and answered the questions.

"Send one of your men back to bring Atwood in and send someone across the river to make sure we don't fall into any holes. Then we'll all cross."

Tomanaga came up to Rossen from the other side of the village, his face expressionless.

"Goddamn it, Tomanaga. What's eating at your ass? You haven't said a word all day and don't give me that inscrutable Oriental bullshit."

Ignoring the slander, Tomanaga spoke with slow measured words. "I told you that something was wrong."

"Well, what is it? I'm not a fucking mind reader, you know!"

"Before we buried Vorhees I took another look at him. I don't think he died of fever. He was killed."

Rossen froze. "Why do you think that?"

"Marks on his throat. There were a couple of bruises on each side of the neck. Not heavy ones, but they meant something to me."

Rossen knew that Tomanaga was master of several martial-art forms and had been taught by his father since he was a child. If he said there was something there, then that was it.

Looking around him, Tomanaga continued speaking more softly than ever. "He was killed," he repeated. "Whoever did it knows his shit. It takes a bit longer than just crushing the esophagus, and you have to be able to hang on, but it works and I doubt if Vorhees had enough strength to resist. That means someone had to keep the pressure on those two points for at least five minutes, maybe a bit longer to be sure. Pressure there stops the flow of blood to the brain and shuts off your breath as surely as though a noose were around your neck."

Rossen began to stammer in confusion, "But, but who?"

Tomanaga shook his head from side to side. "I don't know. But there's one thing for certain, whoever did it is with us now."

Rossen still found it hard to believe. "You think one of Pouk's men . . . ?"

"I don't know, but there are only so many options. You think about it and I'll keep an eye on Atwood."

Further discussion was halted by the approach of the rest of the party.

Atwood looked sullen, tired, his face a patchwork of scabs, scars, and bright new skin exposed to the rays of the sun. He was uncomfortable and wanted everyone to know it.

"I have got to rest or I'll never make it."

Rossen didn't have to make the decision of whether to give him a rest or not, it was made for him. Pouk grabbed him by the arm and pointed into the sky. Another one of the Russian Hip-8 helicopters was heading their way at about two thousand feet.

"Everyone into the hooches!" he cried. Pouk translated. Dragging Atwood, Rossen crawled under the floor of the nearest longhouse, push-ing Atwood's face into the earth. He tightened the slack in his rifle sling, adjusting it so the weapon was snuggled up around his arm. Ad-justing the scope, he sighted on the Hip, praying they hadn't been spotted. This was not a good place to be caught. There was nowhere to run that didn't have an open space in front of it. *Goddamn it!* He cursed himself for being shortsighted, thinking, If we only had even one of those fucking RPGs left, we'd have a decent chance if that fucker hits us.

Inside the Hip, the pilot approached the village carefully, taking his time. If anything happened to his machine, he would be in a great deal of trouble. If he had on board the latest sensing devices, it would have made things much easier and surer, but the North Vietnamese's Soviet sponsors were a bit stingy where certain equipment was concerned, their own needs in Afghanistan taking priority. Still, his machine was a potent vehicle, rockets, machine guns, well armored.

Orbiting the village at an altitude of two thousand feet, he began to slowly tighten the circle, his crewmen keeping a sharp eye out. Coming down to a thousand feet, the pilot thought he saw a dark shadow move beneath the poles of a broken-down longhouse.

*   *   *

Atwood considered making a break for it and running into the open when the Hip began to circle the village. He changed his mind. Those on board the helicopter might not be able to tell the difference between him and his would-be rescuers. Too dangerous for now; it was best to just be still.

Rossen wished he had one of Stroesser's .50-caliber rifles and just one round. He'd put an end to this shit in a hurry. But wishing wasn't going to change things.

Wary, the plot manuevered his craft closer. Best to play it safe: Setting back a couple of hundred meters, he fired a single rocket into the longhouse. The fragile structure erupted. Anxious, he watched and waited. Nothing moved. Content that if there had been anyone down there they would have broken from cover when he fired the rocket, he tilted the nose slightly forward and climbed back to two thousand to continue his sweep, reporting by radio that there was no sign of the raiders at the village of Veng Yam. Only the dead were still in residence.

Ears ringing from the explosion, Rossen and the others crawled out from the houses and ditches in which they had taken cover. Pouk had lost another man. They could be thankful that the Mnong had enough sense and experience not to blow their cover when the single rocket was fired. That left him ten actives out of the original twelve men who had begun this odyssey. In conventional terms, when an army lost 10 percent of its effectives it was considered to be unfit for combat.

Sixteen

As soon as the Russian chopper had moved out, Rossen pushed them across the stream, wading through thigh-deep brown water. He had to put Atwood on his shoulders; the man kept falling. He didn't have enough strength to fight the current. Once on the other side, they moved out, heading for the trees as Seng Pouk said prayers to the gods of his fathers for the spirits of his fallen men, regretting that he was not able to honor their spirits in the traditional manner nor take their bodies home with him to be laid at rest in their family funeral grounds.

They had just entered the treeline on the east side of the stream when the Hip came back overhead. Everyone dropped into the brush to conceal themselves. All except Atwood. Seemingly disoriented, he stood up, actually stepping out onto a small cleared area where sweet potatoes had been grown in a family plot.

"That tears it. Tommy, get Atwood and move out. I'll draw the gunboat's attention. Pouk, you and your people go with him!"

Jubilant, the pilot radioed the information back. "I have located them. They are just west of the village of Prey Tong. Notify Colonel Cao Lam Phang of the sighting. I shall stay on-site and try to keep them under observation for as long as possible, but hurry, my fuel is limited. I can remain on-site for only a few more minutes."

Tomanaga snatched Atwood's arm with his good hand, drawing him back into the cover of the jungle canopy.

Rossen moved to the north, where he could see the Hip coming back. Leading the chopper by twenty feet, he sighted on the Plexiglas windshield. Firing rapidly, he got off three quick rounds, then moved away as the earth where he had taken his shots erupted. A tree the thickness of a man's body exploded. Rossen rolled for the protection of a fallen log, burrowing his body beneath it. The Hip passed over, spraying the area with machine-gun fire, then hovered as the crew inside searched the ground below. Then it began another sweep.

Rolling out from under the log, Rossen fired again, emptying his magazine trying to get off a lucky shot that would hit the hydraulic lines running to the rotor system. No luck, but it did bring the Hip back his way. Once more he burrowed deep under the log.

The message was quickly relayed to Phang in the field, who almost shouted with glee. It was no more than fifteen kilometers to the village. He ordered his radio operator to contact any other aircraft or helicopters on patrol and divert them to the village to relieve the Hip-8. The pressure had to be kept on. With his vehicles he could be on-site in less than twenty minutes.

Rossen covered his head with his arms, trying to hold back a cry of pain. Splinters peppered him. One, the thickness of a forefinger, dug into his back under his right shoulder blade. The decayed log shuddered as if alive under the hammering of the chopper's machine guns.

Hovering just above the trees, the pilot swung his craft back and forth. He knew the enemy was down there and he'd stay on them as long as possible.

Rossen was pinned down. The chopper's blades blew cyclones of dust and leaves around him as the machine guns searched for the softer tissue of his body.

Suddenly, it was quiet. The silence was painful after the roaring of the chopper blades and rattling of the machine guns. The Hip was gone. Rossen didn't stop to wonder why. Ignoring the splinter in his back, he rolled out from under his log and began to run. His back felt as though it were on fire. Blood ran freely, the open wounds from a dozen or so splinters filled with salt sweat stinging him into greater efforts.

Chest aching, he ran west; lungs laboring, his legs were hot lumps of lead. He pushed himself, knowing that he was leaving a trail but there was no time to try and cover his movements. Once he reached Tomanaga, they'd have to resort to evasive actions again. Right now he needed distance. As he ran along the thin animal trail, his eyes filled with sweat, nearly blinding him. He didn't see the man who stepped out in front of him on the trail.

Holding him down on the trail, Tomanaga yelled at him, "It's me. It's okay now." He had been waiting and Rossen had run straight into him.

Sucking great gulps of air, Rossen groaned, "Get off me, goddamn it."

Hauling himself back to his feet, Tomanaga gave Rossen a hand. Bending over to pick up his rifle, Tomanagna saw his partner's back. The fabric stuck in patches clotted with dirt and blood. "Hey! You got hit back there."

Rossen bobbed his head, still trying to save his breath. "Yeah, splinters. Not so bad. No time now. Later take 'em out."

Rossen accepted a pull from Pouk's canteen, grateful to let the tepid iodine-tasting water run down the parched, dried membranes lining his throat.

Hacking out a goober, Rossen cleared his throat, and glanced around at the survivors' faces. "Okay, we're in the shit now and we have got to make time and be careful not to leave any sign. That chopper has sent out the word and the dinks are gonna be on our asses like ugly on an ape." Stopping to take another drink, he eyed the men around him. The Mnong weren't in bad shape and he knew that he and Tommy could still get on with it.

"Atwood. How are you holding up?"

The traitor didn't like the way Rossen and

the Jap were looking at him. Maybe he had been playing it wrong.

"I'm feeling better. I can go on. Don't worry. I'll keep up. I have to. This is my only chance to escape."

"Good enough. I'm going to put you between Tommy and Pouk. They'll help you out when you need it. Okay, let's move it out!"

Pouk put one of his men on point and took the next spot in the line, with Atwood behind him. Rossen brought up drag.

They weren't two minutes on the move when the throb of helicopter blades brought their eyes up to the sky, straining to see through the jungle canopy. They had company again.

Colonel Cao Lam Phang gave the handset back to his RTO. "We have them spotted again."

Taking out a topo map, he examined the area. If the raiders kept moving to the west, they would have to stay in the trees to avoid the helicopters. If they did that, they would be channeled in a controllable area. In this sector the forest was a strip running from one to three kilometers wide with wide-open fields on the northern and southern flanks. Dirt roads ran along the side of the trees. That was good—he would be able to take his convoy and get ahead of them or, possibly, if the helicopters could maintain surveillance, make contact with them in a matter of minutes.

He had them. In his own command he now had an armored personnel carrier, his own jeep, and two trucks filled with soldiers. He would have them, he was certain of it; all that was lacking now was the exact moment. From the south, other units were advancing; he would take his patrol along the northern edge of the forest.

Several times they got a look at the new shadow. This time it was an American Uhlb. A Huey. One no doubt left over from when the Saigon government fell and the North Vietnamese inherited an entire air force by default. It, like the Hip, was painted a yellowish shit brown.

Rossen knew they had been spotted. The son of a bitch stayed too close to them and there wasn't anything they could do about it. Pouk had told him they had to keep moving to the west; there was open ground to the north and south. They were being herded.

The only good thing happening was that Atwood seemed a lot stronger. He was moving on his own most of the time. Rossen was keeping a close eye on him. If Tomanaga was right, they had a traitor with them and he didn't have any idea who it was. But he was not going to let his only MIA get offed if he could help it, and Tomanaga was going to stay next to Atwood all the way to Thailand.

The earth shook once, then again and again.

"Mortars!" Rossan cried as he hit the deck, taking cover behind a tree trunk. More rounds came in. Two of Pouk's men went down. Rossen saw one of them take the full blast from the shell. It tossed the man into the air in two pieces, shrapnel tearing him apart at the abdomen. When he hit the earth, his body was smoking, his separated limbs trembling, fingers opening and clenching, his jaws opening then snapping shut as he tried to scream. Then he was still.

"Goddamn it to hell. This is enough! Tommy, get them up and moving. I'm going to slow them fuckers up or we'll never make it out of here. Pouk, where can we meet later?"

Dragging Atwood up by his arm, Pouk ignored the groan of pain it invoked. "At the west end of the jungle there is a stream. Go south till you reach where it splits!"

"Got it. Tommy, get 'em going. I've got things to do here!"

Tomanaga didn't wait to ask what. There was no time for it. He did as he was told, screaming at the rest of the group to get on their feet and move away from the bracketing 81mm mortar shells.

Rolling over to his back, Rossen concentrated on the incoming rounds, the sound of their whine, until he had the direction. They were coming from the north. Squinting, he saw one of the rounds come in. It was a high arc. That meant the mortar crew was not too far away; they were using a lot of elevation.

Bending at the waist, he moved to the north, the pain in his splinter-infested back forgotten as adrenaline began to pump strong and heavy through his veins.

Tomanaga kept them moving. The mortar shells came after them for a couple of hundred meters, then stopped for a minute before coming in again. The Huey overhead was doing a damned good job of spotting.

Cao Lam Phang gave the fire directions personally, taking the reports from the helicopter then calling out the range and number of charges to the two mortar crews which had been riding in the trucks.

The target was less than half a kilometer away. Easy meat. He would stay on them, pounding at them from a safe distance and, with luck, killing some of them. Another report from the Huey. The targets were up and moving again. He adjusted the range and azimuth. Once they were out of range, he would head back into his vehicles and pursue them again, getting a bit ahead of them and then striking once more with his mortars.

Another report. The target was lost, but he had the direction. They had no choice, he would find them again a bit farther on. Every minute gave him more control over them.

"Load the mortar back into the truck. We're going on. But prepare to set up again immediately upon my command!"

When the break in the shelling came, Rossen thought he had it figured. The dinks were going to leapfrog ahead, then hit them again as soon as the chopper gave them another fix. He ran to the northwest, hoping to intercept them. When he hit the dirt road, he thought his heart was going to burst from the strain. Quickly, he sized up the situation and gained control of his breathing, forcing the air to go in and out of his nose. He listened: There were motor noises to the east.

Searching for a shooting site, he found one a few meters farther to the west. This was going to have to be played a bit differently. He had to take out the vehicles. That was their only chance.

Selecting a site where he could see a stretch of the dirt road long enough to have most, if not all, of the enemy transport in view at the same time, he settled in. He put magazines by his hand, wiped off the lens of the scope, and then did the same to his eyes and face. It didn't take long.

Cao Lam Phang had taken the lead in his jeep. Normally, Rossen would have blown the son of a bitch's shit away, but he wanted the jeep—not the man. It passed, followed by the APC. That puckered his ass a bit, but the things weren't much good by themselves.

They were all on the open stretch when he fired. A single shot blew Phang's driver's head off, scattering brains over the windshield. The jeep went off the road, running head-on into a tree trunk and throwing Phang out, nearly knocking him unconscious from the concussion when he did a somersault and landed flat on his back. The next shot hit the front tire of the first truck; then Rossen took the rear one out with a round through the radiator. The APC went off the road, crashing into the treeline, its personnel searching for the sniper and not having any idea at all of where he was. Their machine guns tore out clumps of brush and blasted holes in the soft boles of banana palms.

The armored personnel carrier wasn't much of a threat—it went out of sight chasing whatever shadow its commander thought he had seen. Rossen turned his attention to the men in the trucks.

The first truck had turned over on its side when the driver, unable to control the vehicle, had gone into a small drainage ditch. Rossen went for the gas tanks. It took three rapid rounds before the tank exploded with a satisfying black, flaming gout of smoke. The insides of the truck began to explode and mortar shells and grenades were heated almost instantly to flash point. That took care of most of the infantry, the men in the trailing truck.

Switching to full auto, he sprayed through the canvas sidings. His efforts were rewarded by screams of pain. Those who weren't hit by his barrage unassed in a hurry, scurrying to the ditch on the north side to take cover. He let two of them hold a round each in the back.

Enough was enough. Now he had to break contact and get the fuck out while he could and before the idiot in the APC came back.

Cao Lam Phang struggled back to his feet, picking an RPK with a drum magazine on it which had also been thrown from the jeep. He gave it only a cursory glance. The driver was obviously dead. His RTO was also dead, his neck angled so that his head looked back over his shoulder.

Not waiting, he dodged across the dirt road into the trees. Stopping, he listened to the firing. There was only one man out there. Good enough. One to one. He would play those odds. He wanted to yell out to his men to lay down covering fire—he could get behind the sniper—but knew that if he did he would give away the advantage he held. He would do it on his own. Those stupid peasants were not much use to him anyway. They would probably end up shooting him instead of the sniper.

Phang was not a coward. He knew what he was doing. Smoothly, silently, he moved a bit farther into the trees. When the sniper broke contact with the convoy, he would once more have to head to the west and Phang would be waiting for him. He wasn't the only one who knew how to set up an ambush.

Seventeen

Breaking contact, Rossen moved out fast and low, away from the ambush site. He'd done all he could there. To hang around even another minute was to risk getting his ass shot off and that wouldn't help anybody.

He kept his eyes centered, not up, not down, just centered; a trick allowing him to take in everything as he ran. God, it seemed that all he had done this day was run. He was grateful for the time in the Rockies—it helped some to get his legs back.

His right foot slipped on a half-rotted patch of leaves. Reaching to steady himself by grabbing a narrow tree trunk, he jerked his hand back just before touching it, taking the fall instead. The trunk of the tree splintered. It broke in half, falling toward him. He rolled away from it, avoiding the sap which oozed like creamy white blood from its wounds. A fire tree. The sap would blister any part of the body it touched.

Phang cursed his luck. He'd had a clean shot at the man, and the fool picked that incredible time to get clumsy and fall. No matter . . . he would have him. All he had to do was keep him pinned down until help arrived.

Rossen was pinned and good. He couldn't raise up to get a shot. Crawling on his belly, he slid into a batch of brush as bullets passed overhead close enough for him to hear the sonic crack. Once in the brush, he heaved his body up rapidly enough to get off a quick burst in the direction of the machine gunner. Then it was back down and eating dirt. The man nearly got him again. Whoever it was on the gun was pretty damned good. He still didn't have a fix on him. A grinding roar growing closer brought a rush of fear chills over his body. The APC was coming back his way. Directly in front of him was a clump of arm-thick bamboo. It burst open as the armored beast broke through it. The machine passed right in front of him, its machine guns still firing random bursts.

Phang screamed at the armored carrier, trying to get the driver's attention. The fool was deaf. The behemoth passed on, crushing small trees. It locked its right tread and swung around thirty degrees to head back to the road, oblivious to Phang's curses and threats. Then it disappeared, leaving him alone to deal with the sniper. He fired a short, three-round burst, where he had last seen the American. The APC had obscured his vision for only the space of a heartbeat.

A red-hot hammer struck him, knocking him around. The bullet had hit his rib cage, breaking two ribs, then ricocheting off. As he spun he saw the sniper. The man had moved behind him and was coming at him, his weapon held at the hip. He went down, his legs having no strength; the bullet didn't kill, but it had enough shock factor to take all of his strength out of him.

Rossen charged forward, ready to finish off the machine gunner. His finger was taking up the trigger slack when he saw the insignia on Phang's red collar badges. A colonel. Maybe he would have some luck today.

Phang looked up to see the American standing over him, the bore of the M-14 seeming incredibly large.

Defiant, his hand to his wounded side, he spat out excellent English, surprising Rossen. "Go ahead, shoot. You can kill me but Atwood—you will never get away with Atwood alive. He'll never talk to . . ."

He left the statement unfinished. It hit him that he had said too much. It must have been the shock of his wound.

Rossen let off the trigger slack. It wasn't what the Viet colonel had said, but the manner of his saying it. It bothered him.

Snapping his rifle up, he fired twice, then twice more, hitting two of Phang's men. Those who survived the ambush were moving into the jungle.

Making up his mind in a hurry, he decided to try for it. There was always the possibility that he might be able to trade the Viet officer if they got in another bind. And there was also the puzzle of what he had said or what he hadn't finished saying.

Jerking the smaller man up by the collar, he pushed him in front of him. "Move out, you dink son of a bitch. I'm not going to carry you. If you go down I'll gut-shoot you."

He forced Phang away, heading deeper into the trees. Once he was where he couldn't hear the sound of any more pursuit, he stopped long enough to take Phang's belt and make a leash with it. He had to play catch-up again, and he wasn't wasting any time worrying about the health of the Vietnamese officer. Phang tried to slow him, but that only resulted in having his breath cut off time and again. He gave up and kept pace with the bigger man. His body was wounded, but most of the shock had passed and his mind was working clear and sharp again. This could be the best way. The American was going to take him to Atwood. With Atwood's help he might succeed in his mission yet.

Behind them, the Vietnamese soldiers halted. They didn't know what to do. Their new leader was the commander of the APC, a sergeant and a fool. With no officers to make a decision for them, it was with a sense of relief they went back to the ambush site to care for their wounded and wait for someone to come and give them orders. It was dangerous in the jungle.

When the pilot of the Huey couldn't make contact with the ground party, he decided to break off the surveillance and look for them.

Once he was off their ass, Tomanaga and his party made good time, using the opportunity to put more distance between them and the chasers. They came to the stream Pouk had spoken of. Staying to the jungle side, they moved south to where it split, and took cover to wait for Rossen. They had heard the firing and the explosions in the distance. Pouk wanted to ask Tomanaga if he thought the Phü Nhām would make it. He didn't. He knew the question would not be welcome.

Rossen gave his prisoner no slack. Any stumble or hesitation and he'd jerk the end of his leash hard enough to bring out a cry of pain. Bringing back a full colonel was a definite bonus. He might be able to answer some questions about other MIAs, but he wasn't going to risk anything by keeping the man alive one extra second if he jeopardized the rest of them in any way.

Reaching the stream, he turned south, taking the same route as Tomanaga and Pouk had. This time he wasn't knocked down when he caught up to them. Tomanaga stepped out well in front of him and waved him on. They had taken refuge in a thick cluster of bamboo growing by the water's edge.

"What the hell have you got there?"

Pushing Cao Lam Phang in front of him, Rossen grinned. "I brought you some company."

Atwood went pale, and his heart missed a beat when he saw Phang. If he hadn't been sitting, he would probably have fallen on his face. His legs had turned to water.

Phang went to his knees facing Atwood. Their eyes met. Ever so slowly, Phang moved his head from left to right. Atwood felt his heart regain its normal beat. Phang had said nothing and now that he had an ally, they might have a chance of getting free.

Pouk looked across the stream. "We had best be moving on if you're rested enough. We still have a couple of hours of light. It is best if we go now."

Groaning with the ache in his legs, Rossen got back up. "Okay. Let's do it again. Pouk, tell your men that I want to get this man back alive if possible, so tell them not to cut his head off just for breathing loud. He could be important."

They had no difficulty in crossing the stream and putting some miles between themselves and the nearest searchers, whose efforts had lost all coordination. They stopped only for short spells to breathe and eat, then moved on again, always to the west and the safety of Thailand. For three more days they hacked and gouged their way across bamboo thickets and oceans of saw-sharp elephant grass, through rivers and streams. They put Phang to work. If Atwood appeared a bit tired, or they had a river to cross, they'd put him on Phang's back.

It seemed fitting that comrade Phang perform some labor.

For all of them the strain was beginning to tell. Their faces grew gaunt with exhaustion, hollows grew dark and deep around their eyes. There wasn't an inch of their bodies that wasn't sore or swollen by the bites of mosquitoes, mites, and especially chiggers.

When Rossen took his boots off, there was a red, bloody line around his calf at boot-top height where the insects had taken roost to eat at his flesh. The worst of it was the leeches, leeches which dropped from trees or transferred to their bodies when they brushed by plant leaves. They had to be taken off several times a day with the lit end of a cigarette. Rossen especially hated the dark brown blood-gorged little beasts.

Tomanaga kept the job of medic. Every night before dark he'd make everyone swab their assorted bites, cuts, scratches, and suck marks with alcohol or iodine. Infection came quick in the jungle. He was concerned about the amount of antibiotics he had to use on Phang to keep his wounds from becoming gangrenous. Even with them, the wounds were beginning to stink a bit.

They had made good time. Seldom now did they see any signs of the pursuers, and when they did they weren't hard to avoid. It seemed the loss of Colonel Cao Lam Phang had crimped their efforts. Now they were near the frontier, their next greatest danger. The conflict on the border. Their first danger was from themselves. Exhaustion! They were getting so weary that each step was a major effort. They were beginning to stumble, eyes were open but they didn't see.

Rossen had to call a halt for them to rest a full night. They had come too far to make a stupid mistake now. They had to rest. Just one full night to sleep and they would be able to make it the rest of the way. Even the possibility of one of their men being an assassin was too much to think about. Incredible weariness dulled all senses. They had to rest.

Seng Pouk took first watch. Phang, as he had every night, was tied, hands behind his back, feet firmly secured to a tree. The watch had been drawn by lot. After Pouk, one of his seven remaining men would take over. Rossen would be next. The lucky ones lay down, not bothering to make any kind of shelter. They lay crumpled, leaning against trees or lying belly-down, faces cradled in their arms. They felt nothing, not the mosquitoes which sucked at them or the chiggers seeking the warm spots where clothing or boots made contact with flesh. They slept.

Pouk's eyes were burning coals. It wasn't so

bad when they were moving. But now, watching the others sleep, every minute was an agony. He wanted so much to be able to close his heavy lids and sleep as they did. He blinked once to ease the strain. Then once more and his eyes couldn't open again. The heaviness of his limbs and body was too much; he couldn't force his eyes open and didn't have the will to call for help. It took too much effort. He fell asleep.

Phang and Atwood did not sleep. They had waited for this moment. The few times they had managed to speak a few hurried whispered words, they had planned for *now!* Terrible fear gave them the will to keep their eyes open a few moments longer than their captors.

Certain the rest were sound asleep, Atwood began to move, very slowly. For a moment he thought about going into the jungle alone, leaving Phang to stew in his own juice—he had never liked the slope-headed bastard very much anyway. Only the fear of recapture or possibly being killed by the Vietnamese or Laotians if they found him kept him from going it alone.

Sliding on his belly, he crawled closer to Phang. It took only a moment to free him from his bonds, but the moment was incredibly long. He expected one of the sleeping men to wake up at the second he was untying the Vietnamese officer. They didn't.

Phang was free, rubbing his legs to restore the circulation. Coming to unsteady feet, he looked around at the sleeping men. Moving silently to the nearest Mnong, he took the man's AK-47, which lay beside him, then stepped to where his back was against a tree. The sleeping men were spread out. Which to kill first? Or should he try to take them all prisoner? That would be a major coup, but it was too dangerous. It would be easiest to just machine-gun them all.

Slowly he pulled the handle back to chamber a round. The bolt made a soft *shussh*ing sound, then a click as the weapon cocked, waiting for the slide to go forward and chamber the first round.

Even deep sleep couldn't erase twenty years of conditioning. Rossen's subconscious mind knew that sound. Above all others on the face of the earth, it knew the sound of a bullet being chambered in a weapon. His eyes opened. Reactions took over. He began rolling and yelling at the same instant, his hands drawing his rifle to him, finger going for the trigger.

Phang opened fire. He wanted Rossen first. From the hip in the dark his first burst of bullets ate up the ground where Rossen should have been.

The sleeping men were jerked back into semi-awareness. Rossen was in the shadows. Phang swung the AK around, spraying the sleep-drugged Mnong. The slap of bullets hitting bodies was punctuated by cries of pain from those who were not instantly killed. Tomanaga rolled behind a tree, dragging his rifle with him. Two bullets tugged at his tunic but missed flesh.

Rossen came up off the deck to his knees. Not sighting, he fired, the butt of his rifle held against his side. The 7.62mm rounds were shot low. Two bullets hit Phang. One low, just to the left of the inguinal above the hipbone, the other poking a clean hole through his side, narrowly missing his kidney. He was slammed back up against the tree, the weapon falling from his hands. Atwood started to reach for it but was stopped by one short word from Rossen.

"Don't!"

Standing up, his M-14 pointed straight at Atwood, Rossen moved closer. Tomanaga came out from behind his tree, covering Phang. Pouk was going from one body to another, guilt tearing him apart.

His voice as cold as death, Rossen looked straight at Atwood, then at Phang. "You people are going to talk to me and you're going to do it now!"

He nodded at Tomanaga. "Tie up Atwood and check out the dink. I don't want him to die. Not yet anyway. We're going to get some answers."

From behind him came a cry of grief. Pouk bent over the bodies of his dead. Phang had killed three, and two were wounded. Bad wounds in the chests and bellies. Wounds that would in a matter of minutes fester into a burning agony. There was no way for them to avoid peritonitis. Their abdominal cavities would become filled with pus in a matter of hours.

They were going to die, and die very painfully, and there was nothing that could be done about it. Even if they could have been carried the remaining distance, it wouldn't do them any good. All there had enough experience to know when wounds were fatal. Blood coming bright red to the lips in a froth. Lung shot. The gaping holes in backs and abdomens. Gastric acids and food spilling out into the cavity. The tribesmen knew it, too. Their eyes took on a calmness as they prepared themselves to meet their fathers in the afterlife. They accepted death with courage and resolve. Death had always been with them. It was not a stranger or to be feared.

Rossen let Tomanaga go to the wounded, and tied up Atwood, making certain the turncoat would stay put. Then he joined Tommy and Pouk to get a look at the wounded.

Tommy whispered in his ear. He nodded understanding. Placing a hand on Pouk's shoulder, he said softly, "I'm sorry. Would it be better for you if I did it?"

Pouk knew what he was talking about. Silent, not able to speak, he nodded.

"Okay, you go away for a minute and it'll be over. I'll do it right. You know that."

Touching each of them on the face once, Pouk moved away into the comfort of the dark jungle to wait.

There had been too much noise this night already and there was no need to use a weapon as heavy as the M-14 or an AK. The silenced Ruger would do very well.

Then it occurred to him, startling him. He didn't even know the names of the wounded men. He had heard them a number of times but they had never registered. Perhaps it was just as well not to know the names of men you were going to kill.

The .22 sounded its hushed whisper twice and the wounded Mnong tribesmen had their pain ended. When Pouk returned, his dead were not to be seen. Rossen had moved them away and covered them with leaves and brush. Not much of a grave, but the best to be had under the circumstances.

"Thank you, Shooter. That was a kind thing to do."

Rossen knew what was meant. He didn't belong to the tribe.

"Pouk, I would like nothing better than to turn that bastard over to you. But we don't have time now. Those shots could bring us company and I still want some answers from him. Once I get those, he belongs to you if you want him. Okay?"

"Okay." The word was said very slowly.

"Tomanaga, patch up the dink as best you can but don't worry about his comfort 'cause he's going to march no matter what shape he's in."

Pouk led Cao Lam Phang by his belt leash through the jungle. The last two of Pouk's men took first and second position, leading the way to the Mekong River. There was still a good chance the dinks could catch up to them. They had to put down miles before they could rest. Rossen stayed to the rear a few meters, but he never got so far behind he couldn't see the backs of Phang and Atwood. Right in front of him was Tomanaga, his rifle never wavering from the center of Atwood's spine.

There was no talking—they were too filled with rage and a sense of betrayal. When they broke contact, Rossen and Tomanaga would settle down to finding out just what Atwood was and why he caused the deaths of the Mnong tribesmen. One or the other would talk. Atwood or Phang. It made no difference.

Eighteen

They didn't stop until long after sunfall. Mist in the hollows sheltered them. In the trees, birds and other animals settled noisily, irritated by the things below them. The things which didn't belong.

Another cold camp. They were tired and hungry. Rossen had lost at least twenty pounds, the hollows of his eyes were deep and hot, his bearded cheeks gaunt. Uniforms hung limp and filthy, waterproofed by their own sweat and body oils. Only the eyes were bright. Bright with passion. The passion of hate for Cao Lam Phang and more for Atwood, who had been the cause of so much needless death and suffering.

They would have liked very much to have a fire to take away the chill that came every night and set deep in the bones until their teeth rattled and bodies shook as though with malaria or dengue. But there would be no warmth of campfire, there would be no light, only the shadows of the trees and the floating mists. Atwood and Phang squatted in the center of the ring. Rossen and the others formed around them.

It was a time for silence, for hate. Phang and Atwood could feel the hate even if they couldn't see it. The mists and darkness hid the faces of those around them but they could hear the breathing, see the body outlines. The hate was real, tangible.

Phang shivered, his wounds feverish and painful. Tomanaga refused to give him any painkillers. Neither he nor Atwood had slowed up their march. Both knew that they were continuing to hang by a thin and weak thread to the life in their bodies.

Phang was changing. There had been a moment when first captured that he was ready to die, but with the passage of hours he found his life precious once more. The memories of how good it was to love and eat, to drink and feel the sun on one's face, pushed all thoughts of social sacrifice far to the rear of his mind. He wanted to live. After all, what would be accomplished by his death? There was no real difference between one political philosophy and another. All worked to the benefits of those in power.

Holding his hands at his sides, he tried to read the expressions on the shadowed features about him. "I would speak to the American."

"I'm here."

Turning a bit to face the direction of the voice, his side spasmed, nearly doubling him up in pain. Slowly, he forced his torso upright. "Let us talk as realistic men. I have something to trade with you. Something which can also work to your advantage."

From the dark, Rossen asked softly, almost gently, "What do you have to trade that I want?"

Phang felt better. The man was going to listen to him. That was important: to begin talking, to communicate. Atwood tensed. Before the words were even said he knew that Phang was going to throw him to the wolves and try to save his own neck and there wasn't anything that he could do about it.

Softly, but with precise expression, Phang spoke.

"What you have here is something of great value to your country. The dog beside me, it is true, was once a prisoner. But he willingly came over to us. He came to us for profit. He has been a long hand for us these past years. As a Caucasian he was able to go where we could not reach and be our hand in areas where we would be suspect."

Rossen hissed at him. "Be more specific."

Phang was pleased. He had the man's attention, and the man was obviously a mercenary who would understand profit.

"Atwood killed for us. Many of those who escaped from Vietnam continued to give us trouble, inciting the people to rebellion and creating many difficulties for us on the international scene. To these people we sent our white dog to sniff them out, then kill. He was able to come and go without hindrance not only in our country but in Europe as well. For every killing he was well paid. I can even give you the numbers of his bank accounts in Switzerland and Belgium."

Phang's side spasmed again, the pain running down the lower wound above his hip. He needed treatment soon or the wounds would fester.

Conspiratorially, he confided, "Consider the

propaganda value of your bringing one such as he back to face public trial. Your propagandists would be ecstatic."

Satisfied that he had made the situation quite clear, he gloated a bit.

"And I can tell them much of what goes on inside the governments of Laos, Cambodia, and Vietnam. We are, as you can see, of great value. I am certain that one such as you would be able to negotiate an arrangement with your government which would enable you to live quite well for the rest of your life. It is something to consider, is it not?"

Rossen didn't respond to Phang's question, instead asking only, "What do you know about any other Americans being held captive? Are there any more?"

Phang shook his head from side to side.

"That I do not know for certain. We who were put in charge of them at the end of the war were never permitted to discuss the situation with anyone, not even each other. I do know that over the last three years I received orders to reduce the numbers of captives I had in my charge. Personally, I do not believe there are any more being held. They would serve no purpose now, only be an embarrassment."

Atwood jumped in. "Hey, you guys. You can't believe him. He made me do it. I was tortured for months. They did things to me with drugs. Fucked with my mind. I'm an American! I fought for my country."

Tomanaga couldn't take any more. He backhanded Atwood across the mouth.

"Shut your fucking mouth, you traitor, before I rip the top of your skull off and let the shit you call a brain run out."

Atwood froze.

"Pouk, how far to the frontier?"

Rossen could feel the Mnong's eyes on him as he answered. "Not far, three or four kilometers, maybe a little more."

They didn't know how Pouk could be so certain of their location but they believed him. The safety of Thailand was only a few hours away. They would make it.

Turning back to his prisoners, Rossen tried to control the anger in him. It had been building and building. Only once had he ever felt such hate, and that was when Tommy lost his hand in Nam. Now this worthless piece of shit he was supposed to bring back was staring at him. And his boss had tried to buy him off.

The mission had turned to shit. Too many good men had died, and for what?

The mist began to lift a bit and Rossen could see Atwood watching him sullenly.

Moving over to squat in front of him, Rossen had to exercise every bit of control he could find. "You know what you are, Atwood? You're a hundred thousand dollars. Do you think you're worth that much?"

Atwood knew that he was a dead man by the tone of Rossen's voice. He found some courage down deep and spat a hunk of phlegm onto Rossen's jacket. Rossen ignored the piece of slime running down the camouflage front. It meant nothing.

"You cost us some good men. You killed Vorhees and we broke our asses to try and 'save you.' Save you," he repeated softly.

The words sounded funny, saving a son of a bitch who didn't want to be saved.

Phang interjected. "I know what your feelings are for this man. But that does not change certain things. Remember this, I am a man with much information. Take me into Thailand and I will defect. I have much information that your side needs. The West will be very glad to have my services. I can be of great value to them."

Tomanaga shut Phang's mouth by placing his hook's point deep into the base of his neck.

Phang froze. Even with the pain he didn't move. He knew where the hook was located and what it would do if Tomanaga applied any more pressure.

Atwood's eyes went from face to face around him. Pouk was impassive, only the beat of his pulse in his temples showed any emotion. Tomanaga and Rossen both had a pale cast to their mouths and around their eyes. Beneath the coating of sweat and dirt, he could see the muscles in their jaws trembling.

Rossen hissed at Phang, "That's right. You're worth a lot. You know things. You'll sell out your side for sanctuary and our side will welcome you with open arms, give you a car and television set of your very own, and all you have to do is betray your own people, become a turncoat. Oh, yes, they'll take you in. Like you said, you know too much for them not to. You will be a rare prize. That's the way our side always works, and yours, too. It doesn't matter what you've done. How many you've tortured and killed. You will be made welcome. The only value you would have for me would be if you knew where other Americans were being held. But you said you don't. Therefore, you're worth nothing!"

His voice lowered to where it was barely audible, the words coming no longer from his throat but deep in his chest.

"You are not welcome here and now. I don't care about what you know or what you can tell. I only know that you are not going to get off."

He nodded at Tomanaga. Tomanaga applied pressure. The point of his hook sunk deeper into the base of Phang's skull, sliding up under the sheath of bone where the skull connected to the spine. The hook went in deep.

Phang felt a burning fire run down his spine as the hook went through the spinal cord. His legs began to spasm uncontrollably as the sharpened point of the hook touched brain matter. Tomanaga placed his good hand on top of Phang's head. Arms straining, he applied downward pressure with it, then began to pull slowly up with the hook.

Phang's mouth opened to scream but naught came from it.

Rossen had grabbed a clod of black wet earth and stuffed his mouth with it.

Atwood watched the proceedings, his eyes growing wide with terror as he saw Tommy sink his hook and Phang's face contort with pain, eyes jerking wildly in their sockets. Tomanaga's face was expressionless. Only steady, calm concentration was shown by the set of his mouth and firm unhurried manner with which he set his hook and began to pull up with the point and press down with his other hand. Atwood thought he could hear the bones separating in Phang's skull.

Phang *did* hear them, until Tommy sucked in a deep breath and focused his eyes on one spot on Phang's skull. Compressed air whistled out between his teeth. Tomanaga pulled up. The back of Phang's head came off, hanging from the hook. Tomanaga held the piece of skull the size of his palm. From it, black hair dripped blood. Phang's brain bulged out of the opening, his face went slack, eyes blank; only his legs still trembled. Tomanaga let him fall over, his face to the dark earth, mouth open. Only autonomic response made him suck in air through his nose and blow it out. Drawn by whatever instinct they have, flies and mosquitoes gathered around the exposed brain, setting down on it to suck at the fluid seeping from the wounded and dying mass of convoluted tissue.

Shaking off the piece of bone and hair, Tomanaga wiped the hook on his trouser leg.

Atwood's mouth was terribly dry and sticky with the sour taste of fear.

"What about me? You are going to take me back, aren't you? I mean, I am an American. I have the right to a trial." His voice rose to a near whine. "Answer me, damn you. You are going to take me back. I'm worth a lot of money to you. A hundred thousand dollars, you said. You can't throw that away. Just thirty more minutes and we'll be in Thailand. You've got to take me back." His voice became a shriek. Rossen stood up and kicked him under his jaw, splintering it.

Standing over the unconscious body, he looked at Tomanaga and Pouk. "It's up to you. Do you want the money?"

Both moved to Atwood's body. Tomanaga and Pouk looked at each other, their faces suddenly very calm; East called to East. With silence they had come to an agreement. Atwood rolled over on his back, eyes misted as he fought back to consciousness. When they did clear, he wished he hadn't. He wanted to scream but couldn't.

Before dawn they crossed over. The Laotian and Viet patrols were easy to avoid. A firefight was going on to the south where North Vietnamese artillery batteries were pounding a Cambodian rebel base. Skirting around a Thai outpost, they picked up a dirt trail leading into Ban Kadon. It was sunset when they reached the dirty, refuse-filled street which served as the main road. Walking through the town, they ignored the glances of curious Thais and Cambodian refugees.

They didn't care what they looked like. Ragged uniforms, lean sallow faces, eyes sunken and weary. The weapons they carried provided them with a clear path through the town. A patrol of Thai border police came by in a jeep. The two policemen started to stop them, then saw the weapons and the expressions on their faces and made a wise choice. Instead of stopping them, they would go to their superiors and make a report.

Weary, they passed through the streets heavy with a mist of cooking smoke and vapors from the night. Dull red glows came from open windows. Vendors still trying to earn an extra baht cried out their wares and made way for the three men with guns. Prostitutes, hair hanging loose, did not call to them from their windows.

Ban Kadon.

Rossen led the way into a ramshackle board-walled tavern. Ignoring the looks of the customers, they found a table in a corner where they could watch the door and have their backs to the wall. When they entered, the talk had nearly died; now it picked up again. From the bar came a blare of American rock music to which diminutive Thai and Cambodian girls tried to dance Western style.

Timidly, a waiter came to their table. Pouk ordered beers and they sat waiting, giving their bodies time to drain of the tension.

The beer was lukewarm, but it was wet and it was beer.

They didn't speak. There was nothing more to be said. For three hours they sat in silence as the customers, either drunk or broke, left the bar to go whatever place it was they called home and wait for the next day. The next dawn would come as it always did.

Rossen's eyes were brought up by the clicking of hard rubber heels on the plank floor. Raising his eyes further, he saw clean-pressed khaki trousers with razor creases in them. At last he saw the smooth, handsome face of Ramasavet.

"Sit down and have a beer?"

Pulling a rickety chair over from a neighboring table, Ram did so. "I have had an alert put out for you since the day you did not come back with Harding. I presume he is dead?"

"You presume correctly."

"Was it a bad journey? I see you have no other guests with you."

"It was bad."

"What do you wish me to say to your employer about the matter?"

Rossen tilted his head back, opening his throat to let the beer flow down in one smooth motion.

Looking at the tight drawn faces of Tomanaga and Pouk, he shook his head very slowly from side to side.

"Tell that son of a bitch that as far as we know, there are no American MIAs left alive in Laos."

Atwood wanted to scream. He needed to scream, but he couldn't. Only gurgles came from his throat and mouth. Bashing his head against the tree trunk, he tried to kill himself but couldn't. He was too weak, and the pain, the incredible pain. It was a hundred times worse than the fire, for it was so slow and it never ended, only worsened with each breath.

His eyes were swollen shut, puffed out ten times their normal thickness. He did the only thing he could and cried inside. He whimpered, begging for death, for someone or something to find him and put an end to the pain. His flesh was being eaten away and he couldn't stop it. How long? How long? It was impossible to tell time, agony had erased all of that.

He had thought the worst had come when Seng Pouk had taken his knife and cut his tongue from his mouth. He hadn't thought anything could be worse but there was. The thin blade of Pouk's knife began to strip away the flesh from his chest, beginning at the collarbones, then slicing down as Tomanaga held him. He hadn't believed he could live through it, but he did. As the limp bleeding flap of skin was cut free at his waist he thought he would surely die. But he didn't.

Rossen stood impassive throughout the proceedings. He would have helped, but Tomanaga and Pouk knew best how to handle the thing which had to be done. For some, death was a kindness and they were in no mood to show any kindness to Atwood. Every second of agony he felt was payment for his betrayals. Every iota of pain was still small interest for what he had done.

Through foam-blooded froth Atwood tried to scream when he saw what was coming next for him. As he had done with Atwood's flesh, Seng peeled the bark away from a fire

tree, leaving the bare clean white pulp open
to the air. Thick yellowish sap came to the
surface of the wounded tree. Dragging Atwood
to it, Tomanaga pulled him up to his feet and
Pouk tied his arms around the tree. At first,
the touch of the peeled trunk was cool. But
only for a second; then the sap began to eat
into his raw bleeding flesh, sinking deeper and
deeper, touching raw nerve endings. Pouk had
tied him so that he had to stand, he couldn't
squat or move away. He was going to em-
brace the fire tree until he died, and death
would be long in coming.

He tried to plead but couldn't, only gurgles
came from his open mouth. In agony, he had
tried to pull away from the tree. He couldn't.
He wanted to beg them to kill him, to please
kill him. But there were no words. Crying, he
touched his face against the white trunk and
the pain increased. Drops of the thick sap
touched the corners of his eyes and burned,
closing them. He blinked, spreading the fluid
around, and the sap ate away at the lenses of
his eyes and closed them.

He didn't know when it was that Rossen
and the others had left to cross the frontier.
He had no thought for anything other than
the burning acid covering his stomach and
chest.

Blisters had formed as large as plates on his

chest and stomach, then others overlapped them and Atwood prayed for death, which would come all too slowly and too late for his mind to appreciate it. Madness was only a breath away and he howled as a dog would, howled silently, and didn't know the reason why. The pain was gone and still he howled and cried and he didn't know why.